Longarm glanced at the girl standing wet and naked behind him and motioned her under the bed. She grabbed a towel and, quickly wrapping it around herself, got down on her hands and knees and scrambled out of sight beneath the sagging mattress and overhanging quilt.

Breathing shallowly, Longarm gained his feet.

The floorboards vibrated as, out in the hall, the three men sauntered toward Longarm's room. The drink-thick banter resonated off the walls.

Longarm pressed his back against the wall left of the door and held the Winchester at port, thumbing back the hammer and snugging his finger against the trigger. He followed the men by their voices and footsteps, until they were directly between his door and the door of Room Nine.

The smell of sweaty, dusty bodies, leather, liquor, and horses tainted the air.

Longarm stiffened, held his breath, waiting.

LONGARM

AND THE
DWARF'S DARLING

JOVE BOOKS, NEW YORK

THE BERKLEY PUBLISHING GROUP
Published by the Penguin Group
Penguin Group (USA) Inc.
375 Hudson Street, New York, New York 10014, USA
Penguin Group (Canada), 90 Eglinton Avenue East, Suite 700, Toronto, Ontario M4P 2Y3, Canada
(a division of Pearson Penguin Canada Inc.)
Penguin Books Ltd., 80 Strand, London WC2R 0RL, England
Penguin Group Ireland, 25 St. Stephen's Green, Dublin 2, Ireland (a division of Penguin Books Ltd.)
Penguin Group (Australia), 250 Camberwell Road, Camberwell, Victoria 3124, Australia
(a division of Pearson Australia Group Pty. Ltd.)
Penguin Books India Pvt. Ltd., 11 Community Centre, Panchsheel Park, New Delhi—110 017, India
Penguin Group (NZ), 67 Apollo Drive, Mairangi Bay, Auckland 1311, New Zealand
(a division of Pearson New Zealand Ltd.)
Penguin Books (South Africa) (Pty.) Ltd., 24 Sturdee Avenue, Rosebank, Johannesburg 2196,
South Africa

Penguin Books Ltd., Registered Offices: 80 Strand, London WC2R 0RL, England

This is a work of fiction. Names, characters, places, and incidents either are the product of the author's imagination or are used fictitiously, and any resemblance to actual persons, living or dead, business establishments, events, or locales is entirely coincidental.

LONGARM AND THE DWARF'S DARLING

A Jove Book / published by arrangement with the author

PRINTING HISTORY
Jove edition / June 2007

Copyright © 2007 by The Berkley Publishing Group.

ISBN: 978-0-515-14310-2

JOVE®
Jove Books are published by The Berkley Publishing Group,
a division of Penguin Group (USA) Inc.,
375 Hudson Street, New York, New York 10014.
JOVE is a registered trademark of Penguin Group (USA) Inc.
The "J" design is a trademark belonging to Penguin Group (USA) Inc.

PRINTED IN THE UNITED STATES OF AMERICA

10 9 8 7 6 5 4 3 2 1

Chapter 1

From the bottom of a deep pit of warm, blissful sleep, Custis Long, known as Longarm to friend and foe, heard someone clear his throat.

The warm tar churned and gurgled around him, and he smacked his lips, groaned, and sank deeper into sleep.

Someone cleared his throat again, insistently. It was like a tug on an imaginary line tied to a hook in Longarm's cheek. Scowling, he opened his eyes.

A flushed, puffy round face hung over him, shaggy gray brows beetled. The man wore a brown serge, double-breasted suit coat with brass buttons, and a paper collar to which a black bow tie was secured. Longarm smelled the pomade in the man's hair, and the slightly musky scent of the gent's cologne.

The man looked vaguely familiar, but in his half-awake state, Longarm couldn't place him. He wondered vaguely why the man was in his rented digs on the shabby side of Cherry Creek.

"Gentleman and milady," the man said in a thick English accent, dipping his chin on the emphasized syllables, "the General and Mrs. Larimer are home."

In Longarm's right ear, someone gasped. *"Oh, my God!"*

Cynthia Larimer lifted her head from Longarm's shoulder, her black, sleep-mussed mane buffeting around her porcelain-pale shoulders. Longarm was suddenly as wide awake as if the gent staring down at him reprovingly—Stanley was his name, the Larimers' head butler—had thrown a pail of frigid snowmelt water in his face.

In a half second, the previous evening came back to him—the opera, the ride home in the rented hack with General Larimer's beautiful niece in Longarm's lap, rubbing around on him, working him into a frenzy. Then the arrival at the gated estate, and the lovemaking, which began in the marble-floored foyer and spread to various rooms of the Larimers' turreted barrack. Except for a couple grounds-keepers and stable boys, the estate was nearly empty, as the General and Mrs. Larimer had traveled for both business and pleasure to San Francisco.

Longarm and the lovely, cultured Miss Cynthia of the raven hair, cobalt eyes, aristocratic jaw, and enormous tits, had laid a fire in the library and fallen into exhausted sleep on the thick grizzly rug beneath a silk comforter and daisy quilt.

Now, the fire had long since died in the broad granite hearth. Golden morning sunshine slanted through the library's three long windows, glistening on the general's polished desk, map tables, Tiffany lamps, and the gold-and-leather-bound books standing straight as soldiers in the floor-to-ceiling shelves.

And Cynthia, her cream skin glowing white in the mile-high sunshine, pink-tipped breasts bouncing, scrambled to her feet, cursing and ripping the comforter off Longarm's naked body to cover herself, however feebly, as she scrambled around the room, grabbing her clothes, which Longarm, in last night's lust frenzy, had strewn from the room's oak door to the hearth.

"Where are they, Stanley?" She was breathless.

"Last I saw, they were still in the main hall," said the butler, standing to one side, a slight smirk twisting his waxed, gray mustache as he slid his eyes between Longarm, reaching for his hat, and Cynthia, tripping around the room plucking up her crinoline gown and lacy undergarments.

"I thought they were gone for the month!" Longarm raked out as, covering himself with his hat, he began stumbling around picking up his own strewn clothes.

"That was their original intention, Deputy Long," the butler said with annoying calm as Longarm and Cynthia scrambled around him. "Mrs. Larimer, however, acquired a cough due to the Barbary Coast's rather inclement weather, and they decided to return home. They arrived in Denver this morning on the six o'clock flier."

The stiff Englishman watched the general's niece with bemused appreciation. He would no doubt remember the sight of Cynthia's naked ass and fine Thoroughbred legs on his deathbed, Longarm dryly mused as he plucked his long handles off the general's mounted elk head.

The butler added, "Fortunate, wouldn't you say, that I'm accustomed to the high jinks the general's absence inspires in these environs, and found you before the general did?"

Cynthia stood at the door, clutching her clothes in her arms. "Stanley, not a word!"

"And risk giving my employers heart seizures?" said Stanley, plucking a garter belt off the gold knob of the map table drawer and extending it to Cynthia as though it were the king's crown. "Uneager to hit the cobbles in search of other gainful employment"—he paused as Cynthia reached for the garter belt, the bunched clothes sliding across her chest to reveal her left nipple—"I wouldn't think of it!"

"Stanley!" The general's voice echoed in the vaulted hall outside the library.

Cynthia sucked a horrified breath and widened her eyes at the butler.

"It sounds as though he's at the bottom of the stairs," said the butler serenely. "I'd say you have thirty seconds, more or less, to vacate the premises."

"Stanley!" the general shouted again, boots pounding on the stairs. The landing was just a few feet right of the library.

Longarm grabbed up his boots and, stark naked except for his hat and the clothes and gunbelt clutched in his arms, ran for the door. "Stanley, there a back way outta here?"

3

"The back stairs drop through the kitchen in which the maids are gathering now to prepare breakfast." Stanley ran his amused gaze up and down Longarm's tall, broad, ruddy frame. "I'm sure the gals would be quite happy to fry you up some eggs, Deputy Long."

Cynthia peeked out the door, then turned to Longarm, the nubs of her pale cheeks brushed with red, blue eyes frantic. "Follow me, Custis!"

She dashed out the door, making a sharp left.

Longarm stuck his own head out.

Cigar smoke touched his nose faintly. Squeaky new boots pounded the oak stairs heavily. A gray head appeared in the broad, shadowy stairwell on the other side of the hall. The general plodded up toward the head of the stairs to Longarm's right.

"Stanley, old chap, where did you disappear to?" The deep voice of Denver's founding father echoed like a bullhorn. "I need some cables sent straightaway!"

Longarm cursed silently, swung left down the dim, high-ceilinged hall between massive oil paintings, tapestries, and occasional side tables adorned with decorative chess sets or antique shields and swords that the general had brought back from Mexico, and ran on the balls of his bare feet after Cynthia.

The girl was a slender, pale figure ahead—her narrow back flaring to tight but womanly hips that in turn tapered to long, milky thighs, her tight, round ass shifting alluringly as she scampered into the shadows.

Behind Longarm, the footsteps grew louder.

Ahead, Cynthia whipped right into an intersecting hall.

Again, Longarm glanced behind.

The general turned at the top of the stairs and strode toward Longarm, angling for the library's open door, light from the high windows limning his grand, leonine head with its thick gray hair and the round, steel-framed glasses perched on his nose. A stogie protruded from his mouth, cigar smoke wafting around him.

"Please don't look down the hall," Longarm silently urged the man.

As the general disappeared into the library, Longarm dashed around the corner of the intersecting hall. Twenty yards ahead, Cynthia paused at the door of her own chambers—the lavish suites that the general reserved for his favorite debutante for whenever she decided to bless him and his city with her delectable presence.

She opened the door, dashed inside, then held the door open for Longarm. He followed her inside, his heart pounding, and dropped his clothes and gunbelt on the floor where Cynthia had dropped hers.

As he stumbled over to the bed, Cynthia closed the door.

"Close one!" She laughed, dropping to her knees with fatigue as the bolt clicked home.

Longarm collapsed onto the mattress. He stared up at the canopy, his feet on the thick-carpeted floor.

He drew a deep breath. "Miss Cynthia, you're gonna be the death of this old badge-toter!"

One hand on the doorknob, head pressed to the door, she turned to him, full lips shaping a grin. She released the knob, dropped her hands to the floor and crawled toward him, breasts swaying toward the carpet.

She had a hungry, bemused look in her eyes as she crawled between his feet, lifted her head, and kissed his cock lolling against his right thigh. "I bet I know how I can reinvigorate you, Custis."

"Not a chance. Not with your uncle just down the hall."

In his mind's eye, a front-page newspaper headline flashed in forty-point type: "DEPUTY UNITED STATES MARSHAL SHOT BY DENVER FOUNDING FATHER!" Below that, in slightly smaller type: "SHOTGUNNED BODY OF CUSTIS LONG—Longarm!—FOUND IN BED OF GENERAL LARIMER'S PRIZE NIECE!"

Longarm tried to ignore Cynthia's wet, silky lips running up the underside of his member.

"Leave me alone. I gotta get to work. Hell, it must be after eight o'clock, and I'm s'posed to be in Billy Vail's office at nine. . . ."

"Mmhhhmmmmmm . . ."

He lifted his head and looked down past his flat belly as Cynthia inched her slightly parted lips back down toward his balls. Her straight, raven hair brushed his belly and groin, tickling him.

He flicked a hand toward her feebly, wincing as he felt his shaft swelling. "Stop. You're gonna . . . gonna get me in hot water."

She nuzzled his balls as she ran her fingertips up and down the insides of his thighs. "I'll protect you, Custis."

She kissed the base of his cock. Lifting her eyes, she smiled at the burgeoning appendage. "What does the most famous lawman on the frontier have to be afraid of?" She closed her mouth over the side of Longarm's shaft. "You're a big, strong boy, Custis Long." Her mouth moved up the shaft, and her tongue flicked over the head. He felt her hot saliva on the tip. "Very big . . . and very . . . very . . . *strong* . . . "

Longarm's heart was thudding once more as she closed her mouth over him and sucked him like an especially tasty lollypop, slowly raising, then slowly lowering her head, her lips stretched taut around the shaft and working his blood up until he bunched the bedspread in his fists, curled his toes, and sucked air through his teeth.

Suddenly, when he was nearly at the height of his desire, she lifted her head, his swollen, red dong flopping back against his belly, soaked in her saliva. "Besides, Uncle George won't come down this way. He knows I always sleep until noon."

He lifted his head and stretched his lips back from his teeth. *"Christ, woman, would you shut up and finish what you started?"*

Cynthia giggled, grabbed his cock in his fist, and closed her mouth over the head once more.

In less than thirty seconds, he arched his back and hoped like hell the good general was far enough away that he

6

couldn't hear his favorite niece at once choking and laughing as Longarm spewed his seed down her throat.

"Custis, will you escort me to Auntie's birthday party tomorrow night?" Cynthia asked a few minutes later, propped against pillows on her bed, which was nearly as large as Longarm's entire rented flat. She'd gathered her thick, black hair behind her head in a loose chignon and, the covers drawn halfway up her breasts, was filing her nails and pursing her rich lips with concentration.

Longarm stood naked at her marble washstand. He was giving himself a whore's bath while staring through the curtained eastern window looking out on the Larimers' rolling rear grounds, dew-damp grass sparkling in the early morning light.

He glanced at Cynthia, brow arched. "Auntie's birthday party?"

"It's tomorrow night at the opera house." Cynthia stopped filing her nails to glance up at Longarm with a sidelong smile. "The territorial governor will be there, and there's a rumor that the president's wife, Lemonade Lucy Hayes, will make an appearance as well."

"Uhhhn," Longarm said, dipping his sponge in the bowl and giving his crotch a brisk scrubbing, "can I think on it?"

Cynthia dropped her arms on the bed with a sigh. "Oh, fudge, you've no intention of going, Custis, and I don't blame you. I don't want to go either, but I have no choice!"

Longarm laughed, toweled himself, and began dressing.

"Oh, Custis," Cynthia grouched when he stood before him in his white shirt, fawn vest, black frock, whipcord trousers, and low-heeled cavalry boots, an unlit three-for-a-nickel cigar in his teeth. "I feel so depressed when it's time to say good-bye to you!"

Holding his hat in one hand, he leaned over the bed and kissed her. He was about to pull away when she wrapped her arms around his neck, holding him there, kissing him hungrily. When she finally drew her lips away, she pressed her nose to his and stared into his eyes.

"You're the only man I've ever felt the urge to marry."

Longarm's balls contracted. He must have winced, for he saw the corners of the girl's mouth turn down. "Now, Miss Cynthia," he said, holding her arms in his hands, "it's far too early in the mornin' for talk like *that*!"

He kissed her again, pulled away, donned his flat-brimmed hat, and wrapped his gunbelt around his waist, adjusting his .44 double-action Colt Lightning on his left hip, butt-forward and slanted toward his belly.

"When will I see you again?" Cynthia asked. "I'm leaving after Auntie's party for Philadelphia."

"If Billy don't have an out-of-down shindig for me, don't you worry, my gal, I'll track you down. If not, I'll see you next time." The marriage talk had frayed his nerves, and he suddenly felt the room's walls closing in, suffocating. . . .

She stared at him, wide-eyed. "Custis, what on earth are you doing?"

He'd opened the window and lifted one leg over the casing.

"I done scouted the outside of your room, in case the need arose for a quick escape. There's a grape trellis out here and, while I haven't done much climbing since I was a mere shaver crawlin' in and out of Miss Suzy Ellis's bedroom window of a night, I think I can make it without breakin' my neck." He winked and offered his patented grin around the unlit cigar in his teeth. "Till next we meet again, my flower!"

"Cust—!"

He closed the window and found a purchase on the grape trellis two feet to the casing's left. He was glad to find that the boards were not overly worn, and would hold his weight. He lowered himself quickly, moving down the ivy-woven slats, looking up occasionally as if expecting to see Marriage itself, like the Grim Reaper, bearing down on him.

The window remained closed, the pane reflecting the climbing morning sun.

What was it with gals anyway? Why, just when the screwing couldn't get any better, did they have to start talking marriage?

Longarm dropped the last four feet to the ground, fell, rolled, and gained his feet in a single bound. Brushing his hands together, he jogged across the open yard to the brick fence, over which he clambered, and ten minutes later found himself riding on the back of a coal wagon heading down Sherman Street toward Capitol Hill and the Federal Building, where his boss awaited.

He hoped Billy Vail had a job for him good and far away.

Longarm lowered his head to light his cigar as the wagon clanked and rattled beneath him, the horse's hooves clomping loudly on the sandstone paving.

Timbuktu sounded about right.

Chapter 2

There was nothing like the thought of marriage to start the day off on the wrong hoof, but Longarm felt better by the time the coal wagon made its way down to the vicinity of the Federal Building. The morning was bright and warm and already the young ladies were out in their summer-weight frocks, brushed hair flowing down their shoulders or pinned behind their heads.

Wagons rattled along the paved or cobbled streets. Dogs milled and the occasional stray chicken or pigs loitered along alleys and vacant lots, foraging for scraps. Birds chirped, babies cried, mothers laughed, Canada geese quarreled along the rippling water of Cherry Creek, and the German street sweepers smoked and joked with passersby.

Fifteen miles west of the sprawling cow town, beyond the stock corrals and the blond prairie grasses, the Front Range of the Rocky Mountains rose like a giant cross-cut saw lying edge up along the horizon. The peak of Mount Evans was still tipped with old snow—its gauzy blue slopes hearkening, beckoning, shouting the right of every man to live as he pleased, unhindered by the bonds of matrimony!

But then, in his mind's eye, he saw Cynthia Larimer as he'd seen her last night, her face hovering over him as she straddled him in the library, riding him like a stallion heading for the far pasture gate, her pale, pear-shaped breasts bouncing behind the tattered curtain of her jet-black hair.

She'd thrown her head back on her shoulders and screamed at the ceiling, "Oh, *Custissssss!*"

Longarm winced and shook his head. Goddamnit. The girl was a plague on him, sure enough. But he had to be strong.

As he approached Capitol Hill and spied the imposing granite block of the U.S. Mint, he thanked the wagon driver for the lift, stepped off the end of the coal wagon, hitched up his gunbelt, and jogged east past street vendors, ranch rigs, and lumber drays, avoiding the choked and clotted board-walks. He tipped his hat to several of the young female clerks he'd grown acquainted with—a younger batch every summer, it seemed—as he took the Federal Building two steps at a time, then made his way up the varnished oak stairs to the door on which U.S. MARSHAL WILLIAM VAIL was stenciled in gold-leaf lettering.

"Mornin', Henry!" Longarm said as he strode into the office and tossed his hat on the rack.

The pasty-faced clerk pounding his typewriter keys kept his nearsighted eyes on the onionskins and carbon in the new-fangled machine's roller, and continued pecking away with strained concentration, his back to the deputy.

Henry sneezed and sniffed. He gave a weary groan, picked up the neat, white handkerchief sitting right of the typewriter, near a water glass and a little envelope of white powder, and blew his nose. He had a miserable expression on his prissy, bespectacled face as he said feebly, "Go on in, Deputy Long. Marshal Vail has been waiting for you . . . overlong as usual."

Henry carefully folded the handkerchief, returned it to its place beside the typewriter, and resumed typing.

Longarm said, "Henry, you look a mite under the weather. Might I prescribe a tall beer with a shot of Maryland rye and a long sojourn to your favorite whorehouse?"

Henry stopped typing. He didn't turn toward Longarm grinning down at him, but Longarm could see the right side of his pale face turn rosy. Henry's thin shoulders rose and fell sharply beneath his starched white shirt, and then his long fingers resumed pounding the odd contraption like those of a professional piano player.

Only, the sound they evoked was far less sonorous.

"Tried and true, Henry," Longarm said above the racket, striding to the door flanking the prissy paper-pusher's desk. "Tried and true!"

He knocked once on the door's scalloped glass, opened the door, and stepped into the office just as Billy Vail loosed an explosive sneeze, blowing paper off his massive desk.

Closing the office door, Longarm turned to his pudgy, balding boss. Marshal Billy Vail sank back in his swivel chair, doughy cheeks flushed as he swabbed his nose with a red polka-dot handkerchief with one hand while holding a fat, wet cigar in the other.

"Ah, not you too, Billy!"

"Ah, Christ." Billy Vail blew his nose. "Nothin' worse than a summer cold." He tossed the handkerchief onto his desk and puffed the stogie, adding smoke to the thick blue cloud already webbing around his head.

"That cigar ain't helpin' any, Billy," Longarm said, sinking into the red Moroccan leather chair angled before the chief marshal's desk, which was buried under ledgers, folders, and portfolios of all shapes and sizes and stacks of paper held together with metal clasps. "Like I was just tellin' Henry, what you need is a tall beer, a shot of Maryland rye, and a long sojourn to your favorite whorehouse."

"Quit trying to corrupt Henry. Good advice for me—about fifteen years ago, that is." Vail shook his head and took another puff from the stogie. He spoke as though from the bottom of a deep pit. "Don't ever get married, Custis. It'll turn your balls to raisins."

Longarm chuckled and looked down. He must have acquired a pensive expression, because Billy shifted in his squawky chair and said, "Let's see, you've been fucking General Larimer's niece for about six months now." He tipped his head back and fingered his chin. "Hmmmm . . . six months. Yep, she must be humming wedding hymns."

"How'd you know?"

Vail laughed. "Marry her, you dunderhead. You know how much the Larimers are worth?"

"And ruin the slap and tickle?"

"Good point. But you know, Custis"—the chief marshal sniffed, took another puff from the stogie, and narrowed one red eye at Longarm across his massive desk—"if her uncle finds out you two have been using his prime digs up Sherman Avenue for a fuck crib, there'll be hell to pave and no hot pitch."

"I feed on the danger."

"You're a fool, but I reckon I might as well get all I can out of you *while* I can." Vail leaned forward, plucked a manila folder from the middle of a stack to his right, set it atop the stack, and opened it. "But this one's easy. Consider it a vacation . . . for both of us, since I'm still trying to count up all the bodies from your last mission. You ready?"

"Shoot."

"You're to deliver a subpoena to a murder witness in Coyote Flats, up Dakota way, and bring her back to Chugwater, Wyoming Territory. That's where the trial's set to start in five days. Your old pal, Jim Friendly, has been lookin' high and low for this gal, accordin' to his cable, and of course he needs a federal badge-toter to haul her back across territorial lines."

"Coyote Flats," Longarm mused, pulling a half-smoked cheroot from his shirt pocket. "I was hopin' for somethin' a little farther out in the high and rocky—say Costa Rica—but I reckon Dakota will do." He scratched the sulfur-tipped lucifer to life on his thumbnail and touched the flame to the cheroot's crumbling end. "Where am I s'posed to find this gal, Billy?"

"She's a showgirl—a singer and dancer—so I reckon you'll find her in a saloon. But you'll have to get the details from Friendly in Chugwater. Jim only sent the cable yesterday, and it was pretty sketchy. Had an air of desperation

14

about it, though I can't say exactly why I think so." Vail sat back in his chair and drew a reedlike breath, curling his nose and slitting his eyes, primed for another sneeze.

"Henry's got your traveling papers. You'll take the train to the end of the line in Chugwater, then the stage to Coyote Flats on the other side of the Dakota line. Now get outta here"—Billy jerked his head down, and his sneeze rocked the room, blowing another sheaf of papers off the desk and making his unoiled chair squawk raucously—"and let me die in peace, will you . . . while I go over the reports from your last debacle."

"Sure you wouldn't consider that beer and rye, Chief?"

"The flier heads north at eleven. Don't go getting entangled with Miss Larimer between now and then and miss it, as you're prone to do."

Longarm had gained his feet and was heading for the door, his cigar in his right hand. "I have no intention, Chief."

"And Longarm?"

Longarm stopped at the door, his left hand on the knob.

"I saw that gleam in your eye when I mentioned this witness you're to pick up was a showgirl," Vail said beneath thin, beetled brows.

"Pshaw!"

"She's no doubt pretty, but judging by Friendly's brief cable, she's also an *unfriendly* witness. So don't let your guard down . . . or your *pants*."

Longarm chuffed his indignance. "You're talking to a professional here, Chief." He opened the door and turned toward the outer office, where Henry was still banging away on his typewriter.

"That's what I'm concerned about, Custis," Billy said as Longarm drew the door closed behind him. "So, to put it to you straight, I don't want you *fucking that girl!*"

That last was punctuated by the heavy door thudding against its frame. At the same time, Henry stopped playing the typewriter to scoop a manila envelope off his desk and extend it toward Longarm. The prissy lad's eyes were red-rimmed and rheumy behind his glasses.

But a mocking grin tugged at his thin, chapped lips.

Longarm grabbed the envelope and shoved it into a coat pocket as he headed for the hat rack and grumbled, "Nice to see you smilin' again, Henry."

He donned the hat, tipped it over his right eye cavalry-style, and opened the door. Walking out, he heard Henry snicker as the typewriter resumed its clatter behind him.

As he hadn't had breakfast yet, and the Burlington Flier wouldn't leave for two hours, Longarm went to his favorite bathhouse for a shave and a soak in a sudsy cedar tub, then padded his belly at a chophouse not far from the Federal Building.

When he'd retrieved his packed war bag and Winchester rifle from his rented digs on the shabby side of Cherry Creek—it didn't look like he'd need his McClellan saddle, as he'd be traveling by train and stagecoach—and had informed his persnickety landlady he'd be gone for a week, give or take a day, he made his way down to the Union Station. He'd dallied too long in the bathtub. The train was moving when he boarded, but blinking against the smoke and cinders billowing through the open windows, he managed to find an empty aisle seat in a day coach.

A grizzled gent smelling like a pig farmer dozed by the window, snoring loudly, his nose aimed at the stamped, riveted tin ceiling. Longarm didn't mind the snores, because the baby crying in the rear of the car and the German couple arguing two rows up and left, as well as the general rattle and clack of the car itself, nearly drowned the din.

The smell wasn't much bother either, for the western wind blowing through the windows stirred it around enough that it blended just fine with the smell of diapers, sweat, sour leather and wool, wheel grease, tobacco and coal smoke, and the cow shit emanating from the rangeland through which the train passed, stopping occasionally when one of the bovines themselves wandered onto the tracks to stare dumbly at that massive, noisy thing bearing down on it.

Longarm had perused a newspaper found under his seat,

16

napped through the stop in Cheyenne, and smoked a cigar on a platform between the cars when, four hours after leaving Denver to snake through the chalky buttes of southeastern Wyoming, the locomotive gave a couple of lengthy whistle blasts. The stockyard pens and corrals outlying Chugwater began closing along both sides of the railroad tracks, and then shanties and log cabins appeared.

The hip-roofed, brick ticket office and waiting room appeared atop the cobblestone platform with a final blast of the locomotive's whistle. The report echoed off the depot building, and the pig farmer on the seat to Longarm's right dropped his chin with a jerk, looking around groggily.

"Chugwater, my friend," Longarm said, rising and grabbing his gear off the luggage rack, nodding his head toward the far side of the car. "Pig pens're right over yonder. I hope you're sellin' instead of buyin'—I hear pork prices are up!"

With that, as the train ground to a jerking halt, and after he'd let the anxious cowboys, farmers, immigrants, and drummers funnel out first, he shouldered his possibles toward the front of the coach, and stepped down onto the sunlit open platform.

In the depot building, Longarm flashed his badge, which he always wore in his wallet when he wasn't making an arrest, at the ticket agent, who vowed to watch the lawman's gear while Longarm tracked down Jim Friendly, the local county sheriff.

Longarm would chew the fat with his old pal, Friendly, about the witness he'd been assigned to throw a proverbial catch-rope around in Dakota Territory, then hop the late-afternoon stage to Coyote Flats.

Grateful to be shed of his gear, including his rifle, which he saw no reason to cart around a relatively tame town when he had his Colt Lightning on his hip, Longarm set out for the sheriff's office and county lockup. He was angling north along Chugwater's wide, dusty, sun-blasted main drag, when he stopped to let two beefy stockmen pass on sweaty mustangs.

A sprawling, hell-red building on the east side of the

street caught his eye. The place took up half a square block, and it boasted a big porch and balconies off the second- and third-story windows. Staring, Longarm tipped his Stetson back off his forehead.

"What the hell is that?"

He must have voiced his question aloud. The oldest of the two beefy stockmen hipped around in his saddle to glance back at him. "Best liquor and women in the territory, *amigo*, but don't let it get around I warned you about the, uh, *confabulated* gambling."

He and the other gent chuckled as they rode on up the street to leave Longarm in the middle of the main drag, staring at the vast, barracks-like building which a large sign on the second story identified as THE DWARF HOUSE.

Longarm remembered there being a big freight warehouse on the lot the last time he'd been through Chugwater. Now, however, said warehouse had been gussied up and painted bright red. A large, raised porch had been added, stretching along the massive structure and trimmed with red, white, and blue bunting, torches for night lighting, and Chinese lanterns.

The building looked like something an evil albeit patriotic giant might call home, but the laughter and tinny piano music issuing from inside bespoke mild jubilation. A good twenty horses were tied to the wrought-iron hitch racks, and two or three gents in trail garb stood around the porch, conversing casually, sudsy beer mugs clenched in their sunburned fists.

Longarm's mouth watered. That beer looked damn good after his three-hour journey in the hot, smelly day coach. After consulting his old Ingersoll watch and deciding he had ample time for a beer *and* to consult with Jim Friendly before catching the stage to Coyote Flats, he dropped the Ingersoll back in his vest pocket.

"Why not?" he muttered, setting his hat for the ship-sized saloon.

Chapter 3

As Longarm mounted the porch, he glanced over the dozen or so shingles hanging from posts and tacked around the front door, advertising drinking, gambling, women, good eats, and clean beds. One hanging right of the batwings professed: THE ONLY THING SMALL ABOUT THE DWARF HOUSE IS THE DWARF HISSELF!

Longarm stepped around the men milling on the front porch and peered over the batwings and the sign tacked to the right wing, boasting BIGGEST TETONS IN WYOMING!

As his eyes raked the cavernlike saloon hall before him, he didn't see any tits right off, but he did see one large gentleman in a too-tight broadcloth suit strolling along the bar wielding a hide-covered bung starter, tapping the mallet in his roast-sized left hand with a distracted air, and yawning.

The man's head swiveled toward Longarm, and he stopped behind a couple of pilgrims bellied up to the bar and beckoned. "Come on in, mister," he urged with a slight lisp, hooking his thick left arm once more, the suit coat so tight it looked as though his bicep would pop through the seam. "The dwarf welcomes you! Stranger or no, you won't be a stranger fer long!"

Longarm grinned as he imagined the big man with long,

curling hair and bushy muttonchop whiskers rehearsing the monologue in front of his mirror every night before he went to bed.

"Say, you folks seem friendly." Longarm walked toward the gent, eyeing a tall, thick glass—easily a third again larger than most beer mugs—sitting on the bar. "And who is this dwarf anyways?"

"The owner," the big man said. "He's usually on the premises, but at the moment he's otherwise occupied." He followed Longarm's gaze to the tall, frothy beer mug flanking a plate of cold cuts before a gent dressed in an undertaker's black suit and opera hat. "Would you like one of those, friend?"

Longarm laughed appreciatively. "Does a bear shit in the woods?"

"Elmore!" the bouncer called to the apron behind the bar. "Beer for the newcomer!"

"Comin' right up!" the barman said as the bouncer turned and, yawning once again, strolled back toward the other end of the saloon.

When Longarm had grabbed his beer off the bar and walked away, surprised that the oversized beer cost no more than the smaller versions served elsewhere, he sat down at a table near the front window and tossed his coffee-brown Stetson on the chair to his left.

He rarely bellied up to the bar in strange saloons—a veteran lawman's precaution. He never knew who else in the room might be holding a grudge against him. It was always best, in a saloon and elsewhere, to keep as many folks in front of you as possible.

He sipped the beer and looked around the dim, sprawling digs with a fittingly sized staircase rising to the balconied second story and beyond. There were several faro and blackjack layouts within sight, occupying lantern-lit nooks and crannies, and five men were engaged in poker behind an open velvet curtain.

Those men and about six others at the bar were more than accounted for by the virtual remuda out front, which meant

20

the others were off frolicking elsewhere about the premises. By the sounds of piano music, loud conversation, and laughter emanating from places unseen, mostly above Longarm, there were more than that. If this place were anything like the Cheyenne Social Club just south of here, there were no doubt private gaming rooms as well as lavish cribs in which the sisters of sin plied their trade. A couple of wall placards mentioned a Chinese healer, while another announced a fortune-teller.

Longarm sipped his beer and stared up at a moose head mounted over the bar. A frilly red garter belt hung from one horn, and the moose seemed to have a twinkle in its eye.

Movement to his left caught Longarm's own eye. He turned to see a tall girl with short, black hair, clad in a low-cut, tan gown and several pearl necklaces, peeking at him over a room partition. She smiled and, fingering the pearls, strode around the dozen or so tables toward Longarm.

As she approached, he saw that she was at least half-Chinese, though she was tall for a daughter of Han. And well filled out. Her dress came down only to her knees, and her calves were long and creamy. Her bare feet slapped the puncheons lightly.

The girl didn't waste any time, for she stood smiling down at Longarm for about two seconds, sloped eyes slitted, before she straddled his right knee. She squirmed around coquettishly, then leaned forward, wrapped her arms around his neck, and kissed him.

She tasted a little like opium, but that was the only qualm Longarm had about the kiss. The girl might take a little more initiative than most American boys are raised to expect from the fairer sex, but her lips were soft and sweet, and she knew how to ply them, like a perch nibbling a corn kernel from a hook, to conjure the right response.

When she lifted her head, Longarm shifted uneasily in his chair. She glanced at the bulge in his crotch, then kissed him again. "You take me upstairs, big man, *ja*?"

Longarm blinked. Was that a German accent this Chinese spoke with, or had her sudden kiss unnerved him?

21

She laughed and continued in a thick German accent, "My father was German, my mother, Chinese. They met working on the railroad, but my mother died before I was a year old."

"Sorry to hear that, uh, Miss . . ."

"Call me May, but don't be sorry. Join me upstairs." She tugged on his shirt collar and squirmed around on him some more, sending the heat of her bottom through Longarm's right trouser leg. "I must fill quota, and it has been slow afternoon."

"It's nice to meet you, May, and I gotta admit you've made my list of five best kissers, but I don't have much more time than it's gonna take me to drink this giant beer. In town on business, you understand."

"Drummer?"

"Lawman."

"Oh, I like lawman. Especially one so big and handsome. Look." Grinning so that her eyes narrowed to thin, dark lines, she slid the left strap of her silk dress down that arm, then slid the other one down as well. She straightened her back, letting the dress slide down to her belly.

Longarm stared at her chest, awestruck. The girl was a surprise all the way around, he mused, for he'd never seen tits that size on a girl who looked otherwise mostly Chinese. The orbs sloped down her chest like pale gourds fresh from the garden—beautifully shaped with massive brown aureolas and nipples large as sewing thimbles. They contrasted with the long, smooth neck and fragile shoulders.

Longarm's groin grew hot, his tweed trousers tight in the crotch. "Damn!"

"Come up to my room, lawman. There is no outlaw in this town who won't keep for an hour or two, *ja*?"

Longarm sipped his beer as he stared at the girl's improbable breasts, amazed but trying to keep his lust on its leash. He had to finish his beer, powwow with Jim Friendly, then hop the stage for Chugwater. That didn't leave enough time for fucking this amazing creature. Besides, amazing as she was, he was too prideful to pay for it.

"This is just a hitch in my trail. You see, I'm on my way north to fetch a murder witness, and I—"

The girl's eyes widened. She planted her feet and rose from his knee as though his leg had been suddenly electrified. She pulled her dress back up over her breasts, securing the straps on her shoulders while looking down at Longarm fearfully. Her lips moved, but no words came out.

She wheeled, strode across the room, and mounted the stairs beyond the bar. Her bare feet went slap-slap-slap on the bare wooden steps, her short, black hair shifting around her head.

In seconds, she was gone.

Several of the men at the bar, including the bartender, regarded Longarm with expressions ranging from amused curiosity to suspicious disdain. Longarm felt his cheeks warm. Grinning, he made a show of sniffing under his left armpit.

"I reckon the train ride in this mid-summer heat made me a might whiffy on the lee side." He threw back the beer, draining the glass, then set the empty schooner on the table with a sigh and gained his feet. "Reckon I'll rustle me up a bath!"

With that, he donned his hat and traced his steps through the batwings. He stopped on the porch, glanced behind him. Inside, several of the saloon patrons and the bartender were staring at him and conversing in hushed tones. They seemed to be as puzzled as he was about the whore's strange reaction.

There'd been something about his heading north to pick up the showgirl that she'd found as palatable as rotten fish. Maybe she knew who the showgirl was going to sing songs about on the witness stand, or maybe she'd suddenly remembered her own prior offenses and had decided she didn't like lawmen quite as much as she'd thought. . . .

Longarm adjusted his hat, descended the porch steps, and headed south toward the boxlike, rock jailhouse hunkered on a weedy lot at the far end of town, its shake roof and tin chimney pipe glowing dully in the afternoon light. When he was within thirty feet of the place, he smelled coffee on the breeze.

Ducking under the low brush arbor, he paused to pat the nose of a blaze-faced dun tied to the hitchrack before knocking once on the heavy, Z-frame door. He turned the knob, pushed the door open, and stepped over the threshold. "Jim, that coffee smells goo—"

There was a loud clang and a grunt as three men wheeled toward him, their eyes snapping wide, one rifle and two revolvers cocking almost simultaneously, the bores yawning at Longarm filling the doorway.

"Shit!" yelled the skinny man who'd dropped the coffeepot when he'd clawed his .44 from its holster, wincing as the hot liquid gushed from the pot to bathe his right boot.

"Hold up there, gents!" Longarm threw up his hands. "My hide's just fine without no holes in it!"

The gent by the stove, who, like the other two, wore a five-pointed star on his shirt, stared down the barrel of his rusty Schofield. "Who the fuck are you and what the hell you want?" He glanced toward the deputy who'd had one hip perched on the desk when Longarm had opened the door. "Wes, you were supposed to be watchin' the front window!"

"I just took my eyes off it for a minute!" said Wes, holding his Winchester straight out from his right hip, the barrel aimed at Longarm's belly.

"Simmer down," Longarm growled, keeping his hands raised high. "I'm federal law. Here to palaver with Jim Friendly about the prisoner he wants picked up in Coyote Flats. If you promise not to blow my head off, I'll reach inside my coat and show you my moon-and-star, all polished up and shiny!"

"Do it slow," ordered the gent behind the desk, who'd lowered his old Colt Navy just a hair and was glaring at Longarm askance. What looked like a freshly stitched cut ran across his right cheek for about six inches, sickle-shaped and smeared with pasty salve.

Behind the man, someone chuckled with devilish delight.

As Longarm snaked his right hand inside his coat, he peered into the shadows at the rear of the jailhouse. Four strap-iron cells stood in a row. The chuckling seemed to emanate from the second cell from the left rock wall. A cot creaked as the chuckling rose an octave and a figure moved behind the barred door.

Longarm plucked his wallet from his inside coat pocket, flipped it open, and extended it straight out from his chest, showing the copper badge but keeping his eyes on the cell.

As the three gun-wielding sheriff's deputies gave a collective sigh and lowered their weapons, Longarm watched a squat shadow move behind them. They either had a fat little boy locked up back there—one who laughed like a man—or they'd snared a midget.

Or a dwarf.

The irritating chuckle continued.

"Well, why the hell don't you wear that thing?" asked the deputy behind the desk, holstering his old Colt Navy. "And you ever heard of knocking?" He paused, jerked a look behind him, and snapped, "Shut up, you little fucker, or how'd you like a forty-four-caliber enema!"

The chuckling grew louder, the pitch even more delighted. A raspy, nasal voice rose sharply. "You boys are as nervous as Mormon child-brides on their weddin' night!"

The skinny deputy with the coffee-soaked boot bent down to pick up the coffee pot.

"*Goddamnit*, dwarf! You were told to *shut up*!"

He threw the pot into the room's rear shadows. The little man ducked as it clanged against the bars, then hit the floor with another, duller bark, and rolled quiet.

The dwarf coughed, hooted, then collapsed onto his cot. His chuckles died slowly.

The three deputies, still standing, turned their heads toward Longarm. They all looked pale and mildly chagrined.

Longarm flipped his wallet closed and returned it to his coat pocket. "You boys do a seem a mite off your feed. He the same dwarf from the saloon you can see all the way from Cripple Creek?"

Another chuckle from the cell.

"Sure is," said the deputy who'd been sitting on the desk and, rifle in hand, had stepped up to look out the front window left of the door. He looked both ways, taking a slow, careful gander.

"Expect someone to try to break him out, do you?"

"Yep." The deputy with the scar sank back in the swivel chair behind the desk and picked up a small, hide tobacco pouch. "And we're gonna *be* expectin' it till you can haul the showgirl back here and we can get her to testify at his murder trial."

Longarm hooked his thumbs in his cartridge belt and strolled back toward the cell in which the dwarf lay, a dark lump on one of the cell's two cots. The dwarf lay on his back, his head toward Longarm, his feet propped on the far wall, hands behind his head, his little-boy's shiny black boots crossed on the wall.

Longarm couldn't see much of the little man, but he could tell he wore a white shirt with spats and broadcloth trousers. His head looked like a gourd—large and pale, with thin, sandy hair combed over the bald crown, and mottled with red blemishes.

Longarm stopped about two feet before the door. "Who'd he kill?"

Before any of the three deputies could respond, the dwarf was off the cot and bounding toward Longarm.

Longarm bounded back, automatically closing his left hand around the grips of his cross-draw .44s. The dwarf leaped onto the cell door with a thunderous clang, closing his pudgy hands around the bars, resting both little boots on cross-bars about three feet up from the floor.

The dwarf—he looked like a hedgehog crossed with a gnome, Longarm saw now—glared at him from five feet away. He had tiny, gray eyes pinched down to slits, a nose like a hammerhead, and furry, muttonchop whiskers ending in two saberlike points at each mouth corner. The rings on his lumpy fingers—there appeared to be one on each finger, in some cases two—winked in the late-afternoon light slanting through the front window behind Longarm.

"Who'd I kill?" the beast raged, gray eyes twinkling like diamonds in his broad, suety face. "I'll tell ya who I killed,

26

you big ugly ape. I killed the mayor of Chugwater!" He threw his head back, laughing, while he hung on the door like a bald-headed chimp in a zoo. "I shot him and then I crucified him on the highest butte over the town. Oh, you shoulda seen it. It was *beautiful*!"

Heart slowing, Longarm released his pistol grips and squinted at the ugly creature before him, giving the fat, little beast the thrice-over before turning his head slightly to say to the deputies, "Why don't you just take his word for it?"

"Won't sign a confession," said the deputy called Wes, lacing his fingers across his belly as he stared bemusedly at the dwarf hanging from the door.

"Personally, I wouldn't need no signature," said the shaggy-haired deputy with a pronounced overbite. He stooped to pick up the coffeepot, gave the dwarf a significant look, then turned and walked toward the front door.

"Friendly wants a signature," Wes said as the shaggy-haired gent went out, apparently to refill his coffeepot. "And so does the judge. And since the little cocksucker won't confess, we need that showgirl who witnessed the whole thing to come back down here and sing her song in front of the circuit judge."

The dwarf laughed. He opened his hands and kicked out from the door. He dropped onto his heels, stumbled back a few steps. "What's to confess, gents? I was just funnin' with ya. Take a joke, will ya?"

He brushed off his hands, lifted the right one to his mouth, breathed on one of his rings, and scrubbed it against his shirt. "And I wouldn't count on findin' Amber. I sense somethin' *bad* mighta happened to that girl. She runs with the wrong folks, don't you know?"

He laughed and returned to his cot.

Longarm dug a cheroot from his shirt pocket and turned to Wes. He wanted the whole story, from beginning to end, but he'd rather get it from the sheriff himself. "Where's Friendly?"

"Out to his ranch. Went home for lunch. Hasn't shown back up yet."

"Still on the ranch he was on a year ago—two miles north?"

"Same one."

"Got a horse I can borrow for a couple hours?"

"Got one all saddled in the stable back yonder," said. the deputy standing with his rifle at the window, peering nervously up and down the street.

The man turned sharply to Longarm and squinted one eye beneath the funneled brim of his battered Stetson. "I'd be careful, if I was you. If the dwarf's toughs find out the fed'ral we been waitin' for is in town, they're liable to do to you what they done to the mayor."

Longarm didn't tell him that, after his visit with the whore in the dwarf's saloon, they probably already knew. He just tipped his hat to the man and went out, hearing the dwarf chuckling behind him.

Chapter 4

As Longarm retraced his steps back toward the train depot with the intention of retrieving his rifle, so he'd have something more than his forty-four for swapping lead with possible bushwhackers when he rode out to palaver with Jim Friendly, he glanced at the Dwarf House.

Two big men in three-piece suits and bowler hats were on the porch. The one who'd been so friendly to Longarm earlier stood right of the batwings with a double-barreled shotgun in his crossed arms. The other, who wore a flamboyant red mustache and goatee, sat on the top step, a Winchester across his pinstripe-clad knees.

The gent on the top step was poking a toothpick around between his teeth. Both stared at Longarm with a menacing lack of expression.

Longarm grinned and waved. When neither responded in kind, he shrugged and continued to the train depot, where he picked up his long gun, made sure it was loaded, then picked out a back way, presumably out of sight from the Dwarf House, to the stable flanking the jail.

Ten minutes later, he was threading his way amongst the chalky, bullet-shaped, sage-tufted buttes west of Chugwater. Apparently, the deputy's mule-eared claybank didn't appreciate having a stranger on its back. Every few minutes, it stopped dead in its tracks to stomp its front left hoof and shake its head before continuing.

Longarm didn't mind. The stops gave him time to look around and sniff the breeze for trouble, none of which he found until he figured he was within shouting distance of the Friendly spread.

The horse stopped once more, nickering. Two seconds later, a distant rifle shot echoed. Someone yelled, then two more rifle shots cut the hot afternoon silence.

A flock of blackbirds flew up from a cottonwood strand along the narrow, rocky creek ahead and right of the wagon trail. Squawking and flapping their wings raucously, the flock angled straight up, then back over Longarm's right shoulder.

Longarm shucked his Winchester and, keeping his head low, looked around, ears pricked. The shots continued sporadically from about a half mile ahead, and a girl yelled angrily.

Didn't Jim Friendly have a daughter?

Longarm rammed a shell into his Winchester's breech, then ground his heels into the claybank's flanks. "Come on, old son. Quit fuckin' around and tear up some trail!"

The shots continued with the occasional, accompanying tinkle of breaking glass, the din growing louder as the claybank's hooves tattoed the wagon trail. Longarm followed a wide bend in the creek, then jerked back on the reins and slid out of the saddle.

The claybank continued ahead for a few steps, then, startled by the rifle fire, turned and headed back the way he and Longarm had come, bucking, the reins trailing along the ground.

Longarm dropped to one knee in the middle of the trail. In the bowl-shaped fold in the buttes ahead, the Friendly log cabin hunched beneath a cottonwood—a low, brush-roofed affair with a lean-to addition on the far side. Across the yard was a log barn, two corrals, a small outbuilding, and a windmill and large, round stock tank.

The three corraled horses ran in circles, manes flashing silver in the sunshine, loosing fearful whinnies.

Two smoke puffs appeared in the cabin's two front windows, one each side of the front door, the rifle reports following an eyewink later, one after the other. The shots were answered by two other rifles somewhere near the barn and corral. Longarm couldn't see the shooters, but smoke wafted from that side of the barn, webbing on the lazy summer breeze.

Another shot flatted out over the buttes, louder than the others. It seemed to come from the other side of the butte on the right side of the trail.

Keeping his head down, Longarm jogged back the way he'd come for about fifty yards, then turned off the trail, following a crease between buttes to the edge of the cottonwood-sheathed creek. The shooting continued sporadically, three men in the buttes popping off at Jim Friendly's cabin.

If Longarm could get behind the bushwhackers, he'd even Friendly's odds considerably. . . .

Keying on the nearest shooter's echoing shots, he left the creek and climbed the shoulder of a butte. A mine portal appeared in the ravine to his left, and he remembered that Friendly had first come to Chugwater as a prospector. By the sound of the nearest shots, the shooter was hunkered down at the mine's mouth, probably just inside the portal, from which he had a pretty good view of the Friendly log cabin.

Longarm hunkered down on his haunches to consider the situation. He could cat-step along the butte until he'd brought the shooter into sight below, but he'd have a better chance of surprising the man if he flanked him. From the top of the mine portal, Longarm could bear straight down at the top of the bushwhacker's head as the man stared off toward the cabin.

Longarm straightened, climbed several more feet up the butte shoulder. When he was even with the roof of the mine, he stepped out onto the sod-covered frame. Spindly brown weeds and sage grew thick on the roof of the mine, which Friendly had cut into the earth between two buttes and from which, the sheriff had told Longarm, he'd produced nearly enough color to cover his supply costs.

Squeezing his rifle in both hands, Longarm crabbed out toward the lip of the roof, hoping like hell the old frame wouldn't give way beneath him. He jerked with a start, stopping in his tracks, when the man below him shouted, "Come on out, Friendly! It's you we're after! No point in gettin' your daughter killed!"

A rifle boomed from the direction of the cabin. There was the sound of a bullet tearing up gravel and sod somewhere ahead and below Longarm.

"Shit," the bushwhacker carped under his breath. His rifle boomed, the report echoing around the bluffs and making the frame tremble beneath Longarm's boots.

The lawman took two more steps forward, closing the gap between him and the portal's lip to ten feet. Something rattled in the brush before him. He stopped, looked down.

A thick, stone-colored diamondback lay coiled two feet in front of him, the last four inches of its tail raised, rattles quivering. The flat head was turned toward Longarm, beady, copper eyes regarding the lawman disdainfully, the forked tongue testing the air.

"Hey, who's up there?" came the shooter's voice from below.

Longarm glanced over the portal's lip. The shadow of his hat angled over the lip and onto the ground near the bushwhacker.

Shit.

A rifle thundered. The slug drilled through the roof from below, spitting sod and wood splinters into the air between Longarm and the snake.

The snake leaped toward Longarm's right shin—a gray-green blur of motion.

At the same time, Longarm slashed down and out with his rifle barrel. He caught the snake six inches beneath its head.

Lifting his rifle out away from him, he tossed the stiffly twisting viper over the portal's lip. The snake landed on the

32

ground below with a dull thud. The rattling grew louder, fiercer.

"Hey!" the shooter grunted. "*Ahhhh! Fuck! Goddamn!* Ohhh-*owwww!*"

Boom! Boom! Boom!

Three bullets ripped through the roof in front of Longarm, throwing sand and gravel as high as his head. Another clipped the lip of the portal and whistled over Longarm's left shoulder, angling off behind him.

He bolted forward, snugged his rifle to his shoulder, and aimed down over the mine portal's entrance. Below, a slender man with a broad, flat face, suspenders, and shotgun chaps, lay sprawled on the ground. The snake had its teeth dug into the man's neck, whipping its tail.

The man screamed as he ripped the snake loose, blood washing down from the two deep holes in his neck. He tossed it toward the ranch yard as he took his smoking rifle in both hands and rammed another shell into the chamber.

As the man raised the rifle and jerked his enraged, pain-wracked eyes toward Longarm, Longarm squeezed the Winchester's trigger.

A neat round hole appeared in the man's forehead. The ground behind his head turned bright red. His eyes rolled back. He dropped his rifle, and his head sank against the bloody sand and grass at the mouth of the mine, his legs quivering.

Beyond, the snake slithered into the brush.

Longarm looked at the cabin fifty yards across the clearing. Smoke puffed around the stock tank flanking the hitch rack right of the front door. A hat crown poked above the tank. As reports sounded from the barn and corrals, neither of which Longarm could see because of the steep bluff on his right, chunks of wood were torn from the tank.

The hat dropped out of sight.

Jacking a fresh round into his rifle's breech, Longarm leapt from the mine portal's roof to the bluff on his right. Holding the rifle in one hand, he scrambled up the steep incline, pulling at the brush with his free hand for leverage.

He ran over the top of the butte and dropped down the other side. Six feet from the base, he lost his footing in the slick grass, and rolled to the bottom. Cursing, he bounded off his heels and ran crouching along the back of the corral farthest out from the barn.

To his left, Friendly's horses were still running and nickering. A set of boots and a rifle stock appeared behind the legs of a milling buckskin.

Longarm stopped, crouching and snaking his Winchester between the upper and middle corral slats. The buckskin cantered off to Longarm's left. A man stood there, crouching and aiming a carbine toward Longarm's side of the corral. Paunchy, he wore a vest and bow tie under his duster, a dirt-streaked bowler perched atop his head. A fat stogie protruded from the left corner of his mouth, tobacco juice dripping down his chin.

Regulator, without a doubt . . .

Longarm aimed at the man's chest. "Hold it, friend!"

The man's eyes snapped wide as he jerked the rifle to his shoulder and swung the barrel toward Longarm. Longarm pumped two rounds through his chest.

As the man screamed and staggered back, the horses bolting away from him, a rifle popped on the corral's far side. The bushwhacker's chin tipped forward as his hat flew off his head, in a spray of blood, bone, and brains.

He hit the ground on his back, in the middle of the corral, and lay with his arms and legs splayed, trembling, eyes blinking rapidly. In seconds, his body stilled, and he lay staring skyward as blood and brains continued to ooze from the large, ragged hole in his forehead.

Longarm lifted his gaze to stare across the corral. A big man with a patch beard, high-crown Stetson, red-plaid shirt, deerskin chaps, and suspenders stood resting the barrel of a Spencer rifle atop the corral. His lips stretched, and his blue eyes glittered.

"Custis, I had a feelin' that was you."

"Funny way to while away an afternoon, Jim."

"Wasn't my idea."

Several more rifle reports sounded. A man cursed loudly.

As Jim Friendly turned and ran around the front of the barn, Longarm ran around the rear. They both stopped on the far side of the barn, Friendly at the front, Longarm at the rear. The windmill clattered as it splashed water from a pipe into the large, corrugated tin trough ahead and to Longarm's right.

Forty yards away, near the windmill, a slender young woman in a simple cotton dress, stockman's boots, and man's broad-brimmed felt hat squatted over a man lying on his side, a rifle in the dust nearby. The girl was on one knee, leaning on her Winchester as she glanced at Jim Friendly walking toward her from the barn.

"Got another one, Pa," the girl said huskily. "Deader'n hell."

Longarm had stopped at the barn's rear corner, Winchester extended from his right hip. Now he started forward. He hadn't taken two steps before the girl jerked her head toward him, standing, levering a shell into her Winchester's breech, and bearing down on him from her left shoulder.

"Hold it right there, bucko, or you'll be goin' the way of your *compañeros*!" She slitted one eye as she stared down the rifle barrel, the top half of her face shaded by her hat. "Toe down!"

Longarm stopped as Jim Friendly said, "Ease off, Mary Lou. That's my ole pal, Longarm. He done cleaned the clock of one and half of these potshootin' miscreants, so be good now and lower that saddle gun before he thinks I raised you wrong!"

The girl ran her eyes up and down Longarm, scowling. When she had finally lowered the rifle, Longarm strode toward her and the dead man on the ground before her. He kicked the body over, saw the two holes in his chest still pumping fresh blood.

"Nice shootin', miss."

"You dress right fancy for a lawman," grumbled Mary Lou Friendly.

She was a slender, high-waisted girl, and from her dark

complexion and high, flat cheekbones, she appeared to have some Indian blood. The hair pulled behind her head and secured in a French braid below her hat was black as jet.

"You can thank Lemonade Lucy Hayes for that," Longarm said. "The president's dear wife thinks all federal employees should dress like gentlemen and ladies, and talk as though they've been educated at Harvard. So I hope you'll forgive me when I ask"—Longarm switched his gaze to Sheriff Friendly standing beside his daughter, scowling down at the dead man—"just what in hell is goin' on around here, Jim?"

"What's it look like?" Friendly said as he hunkered down on one knee and began probing the dead man's pockets. "Someone's trying to clean my clock. Mine and Mary Lou's, I should say, and that just damn burns my ass to a goddamn crisp!"

"I stopped at your jail, saw the demonic dwarf you got locked up."

The sheriff jerked a cowhide wallet from the man's inside vest pocket, and peeked inside. "Yeah, it's that little son of a bitch that sicced these three on me, all right. I don't recognize this one nor the one in the corral. And I no doubt won't recognize the one whose lights you blew out over by the mine either. It's just like that little pill to go out of town for his gunslicks, so his high jinks can't be traced back to him."

The sheriff plucked three dollars from the dead man's wallet and handed them up to Mary Lou. "Take these and buy yourself some hair ribbons or forty-four shells, honey."

The girl took the bills in her gloved right hand as she rested her rifle over her left shoulder.

Friendly poked around in the wallet's other compartments. "Just as I suspicioned—nothin' to identify the son of a bitch. Hasn't been paid yet either."

"Never will . . . now," offered Mary Lou, glowering down at the dead man, one boot cocked, her mouth twitching up at one corner.

"Jim, I have a stage to catch in ninety minutes," Longarm said as he replaced the spent shells in his Winchester's magazine. "And I'd sure like to know what this little pageant's about before I saunter into the second act."

Jim Friendly straightened. He tossed the empty wallet onto the dead man's bloody shirt and looked at his daughter. "Honey, would you fetch the wagon and load these bodies up for your dear old pa? I'll take 'em to town later and see if I got any paper on 'em. In the meantime, Longarm and I need to powwow over coffee and bourbon."

"Go on, Pa," said Mary Lou. "I'll fill the wagon with these blood sacks and be in shortly to serve the pie I got in the oven."

"She shoots like Miss Calamity Jane Canary," said Longarm as he and Jim Friendly headed toward the cabin. "How's her pie?"

"Just awful!" Friendly said, slapping his hat against his thigh and chuckling. "But don't let on. That girl is not only handy with a fire stick, she's got a temper like her ma—the full-blood daughter of a Cheyenne war chief!"

Chapter 5

While Sheriff Friendly's pretty, half-breed daughter headed for the barn to hitch up a rig in which to load the unfortunate bushwhackers, Friendly himself led Longarm to the two-room cabin hunkered at the base of an eroded butte.

"I'm gonna have to apologize for the housekeeping," the sheriff said as he gave the half-open door a shove and stepped inside. "Me and Mary Lou weren't expecting company and, as you can see, those dead sons of bitches didn't improve on the natural state of our disarray."

"No problem at all, Jim," Longarm said, doffing his hat as he followed Friendly through the door, his boots crunching broken window glass.

Both front windows were shattered, and glass shards littered the floor, the long eating table, and several cupboards. Bullet holes showed in the back wall, and the clay flowerpot on the table was broken, dirt and a wild blue iris strewn across the oilcloth. The cabin's cluttered main room was rife with the smell of cordite and the apricot pie baking in the iron range squatting against the far right wall.

"Those merciless bastards!" Friendly exclaimed, staring at the bottle lying shattered on a shelf, the nut-brown alcohol still dripping from the shelf to the rough wood floor below.

"I was cursing my luck that we hadn't kept one alive to talk, but now I'm glad we done killed 'em *all*!"

Longarm nodded in agreement. "It's one thing to try perforatin' a man's hide, but to lay waste to good Kentucky bourbon is a capital offense no matter how you look at it." He tossed his hat on the table and ran a hand through his thick, close-cropped hair and sighed. "I'll settle for a cup of java, Jim. If'n they haven't ruined your coffeepot!"

"No need to panic." Friendly was rummaging around beneath the bed covered with a bobcat's fur at the room's right rear corner. He pulled his arm out and held up a dusty, corked bottle. "I always keep one under there in case I have trouble sleepin'."

"You're a good man, Jim. Always said so."

Friendly walked to the table and used his hat to sweep most of the dirt and debris from the table onto the floor. "I apologize again for the mess, Custis. Makes me wanna hang up that dwarf by his little toes and beat him with a knotted rope. The Constitution, my ass! Have a seat."

Longarm pulled out a chair and sat down heavily. "You're sure those were the dwarf's lackeys? We lawmen tend to acquire all manner and number of non-admirers."

"They were sent by him, all right," Friendly said as he tossed his hat onto the rack near the door and grabbed a couple of stone mugs from a shelf. "Of course, I can't prove it. But that little bastard's been threatening to kill me in all manner of ways ever since I arrested him. Thanks for the help, Custis. I owe you."

"Looked to me like you and Mary Lou were gettin' along just fine."

Friendly laughed as he set the mugs on the table and ambled toward the range to fetch the coffeepot. "She can shoot, can't she?"

"You raised her right, Jim." Longarm got out a cheroot and thumbed a lucifer to life. "Now, tell me again who the dwarf killed and why and how the showgirl in Coyote Flats fits into all this."

As he filled mugs three-quarters full of coffee, Friendly

said, "To make a long story short, the little bastard shot the town mayor in his office a few weeks back. Then he had him crucified in the buttes north of town. There were three witnesses—two of the dwarf's bodyguards and the dwarf's mistress at the time, a showgirl named Amber Rogers. That's her show name."

Friendly topped each mug off with bourbon, shoved one toward Longarm, hooked a gnarled finger through the handle of the other, then sat down with a grunt. "A couple waddies found the mayor half dead, just like Christ on Mount Calvary. He lived a day, but couldn't open his mouth but to spit up blood now and then. I think I know why he was killed. He was taking graft from the dwarf to ignore—and to encourage *me* to ignore—his crooked gambling and the illegal taxes he's been extorting from other business owners in Chugwater. His reasoning, as I understand it, is his big saloon brings in business the town wouldn't otherwise attract."

Longarm made a sour expression. "The crucifixion would have sent a right convincin' message to the whole town." He sipped the bourbon-laced, coal-black coffee. "Pay your taxes nice and peaceable like, or suffer some rather painful *consequences*."

"It worked too," Friendly grunted. "I can't get nobody to murmur a word about what they know about the dwarf's evil deeds. The shop owners in Chugwater are as tight-lipped as his bouncers, bartenders, and sisters of sin. Even this showgirl, Miss Rogers, lit a shuck about two days after the murder."

"Why'd she run?"

"I got no idea. You can ask her as soon as you meet her up Coyote Flats way."

"What makes you think she'll come back and testify after runnin' out on you in the first place, Jim?"

"She said she would . . . at least, last time she cabled." Friendly sipped the coffee and sighed. "She sent a telegram about a week after the mayor's murder, said she'd seen the dwarf kill the mayor and was willing to testify to that effect. She told me where she was, that she'd lit out 'cause she was afraid, and that she'd come back as long as I had the dwarf all locked up and could guarantee her safety."

"A showgirl with a conscience?"

Friendly shrugged. "A week ago, I cabled her that I was sendin' a federal lawman up to Coyote Flats to bring her back down here safe. She didn't respond."

"Think she got to thinkin' twice about testifying?"

Holding the cup in both his big, brown hands, Jim Friendly looked askance over the brim at Longarm. "That's one possibility. Another is that the little bastard got to her. I heard a rumor in one of the saloons he's put out a bounty on her. Two thousand dollars."

Longarm drank the surprisingly good java and swallowed, then stuck the cigar between his teeth. "I don't like that particular hitch in the road, Jim."

"Didn't think you would. I ain't partial to it my ownself. And I ain't even the one goin' to bring her back the hundred miles from Coyote Flats."

"If there's anything to bring back . . ."

"Don't say that, damnit, Custis. If I can't put the dwarf away for good—and this murder charge is just what I need, though I can't say I was sorry to see that bastard mayor get his just desserts—he's liable to ruin my town. And *me*, for that matter."

Friendly swallowed a mouthful of coffee and bourbon, and slapped the table so hard a shard from the clay pot that had been hanging near the table's edge clinked onto the floor. "Everything was fine here before he came in his with his little fists full of money from some outlawry he'd done down Texas way. He bought out the old Mason-Mercury freight buildings, turned 'em into a gambling den and whorehouse, and brought in a bunch of outlaws to ride roughshod for him.

"The town's been goin' to hell ever since. A good dozen of our best citizens done already left, and there's been so many fights and killings on account of the gamblin' and loose women, I had to hire two more deputies. Yessir, I hope that showgirl's still dancing on this side of the sod, Custis. If not, my goose is cooked!"

Longarm watched out the window as Mary Lou clattered a battered, green farm wagon up to the front stoop, jerked back on the mule's reins, and set the brake with a rusty squawk. "Hard to believe such a little package as the dwarf has wreaked so much havoc for you, Jim."

"Orneriness comes in all shapes and sizes." Friendly was staring out the broken window as his daughter adjusted one of the three bodies sprawled in the buckboard's box, bunching her lips as she tugged on a foot. The sheriff turned to Longarm, one bushy, salt-and-pepper eyebrow arched. "Say, don't you have a stage to catch?"

"Holy shit," Longarm said with a start. He plucked his old Ingersoll from his vest pocket, and clicked open the lid. "I've got a half hour. Can I make it?"

"You could make it by the hair on your teeth, but I assume you gotta run down your hoss first."

Longarm had forgotten about the deputy's claybank. He cursed again and kicked his chair back six inches before Friendly placed a hand on his forearm. "Why don't you sit tight, start fresh tomorrow?"

"There another stage through here tomorrow?"

Friendly nodded. "Eight o'clock sharp. This country's become right busy since we found gold and screwed the Injuns out of the Black Hills." Friendly jerked his head toward the door and lowered his voice. "I gotta run to town, pull the night shift at the jailhouse with that kill-hungry pipsqueak. Mary Lou can fend for herself all right, as you seen, but I do hate to leave her all alone out here."

"You want me to spend the night alone with your daughter?"

"You'll probably miss the afternoon stage anyways. Even if you didn't, this one circles too far north, takes the long way around the Buffalo Knobs, so I don't see what difference it'd make. I'll buy your ticket, and your office can pay me back later."

Longarm thought it through quickly. He reckoned Friendly was right. He'd probably miss today's stage anyway, and he'd hate for something bad to happen to the sheriff's daughter because he was trying to hop a stage he didn't really need to catch, aside from the fact that Uncle Sam had already paid for his ticket and Henry in Billy's Vail office was going to throw a shit-fit at the complication.

Before he could say anything, the door opened and Mary Lou clomped in, skirts swishing about her long legs, stockmen's boots thumping the floorboards. She stopped with one hand on the doorknob, the other thumb extended over her right shoulder to indicate the buckboard behind her.

"Wagon's loaded, Pa."

"Thanks, honey. Guess what? Longarm needs a place to lay over a night, so I told him he could stay here with you." He gave Longarm a warning, wolfish stare. "Don't you worry none, girl—I done told him you were pure and would stay that way until your weddin' night."

Longarm felt his face heat up as the pretty half-breed turned her incredulous eyes on him.

Friendly stood and drained his coffee cup. "I'd best get to town with those carcasses." He walked around the table and kissed Mary Lou's right cheek. "You take care now, honey, and feed the good deputy well."

He donned his hat, grabbed his rifle, and glanced at Longarm still sitting woodenly in his chair, feeling awkward at the prospect of spending an evening alone with the sheriff's pretty daughter—a girl he barely knew well enough to tip his hat to in the street.

"Custis, I'll hold that stage for you in the mornin', but don't dally. The driver's right persnickety about keepin' his timetable."

"Hey, wait, Jim—I got a war bag over to the train depot!"

"I'll have it loaded onto the stage fer ye, Custis. *Hasta luego!*"

The sheriff cocked his rifle and left, closing the door behind him, leaving Mary Lou standing by the table. She crossed her arms on her chest and regarded Longarm like something her father had tracked in from the pasture.

For the first few minutes after Sheriff Friendly left Longarm alone with Mary Lou in the Friendly cabin, Longarm felt like a bull buffalo in a china closet. He said he'd best run his horse down and put it in the barn, to which Mary Lou fairly growled as she opened the range door, "Best have a piece of pie first, if you've a mind to. It's best fresh out of the oven."

Longarm wasn't really craving a piece of pie, but the girl's gruff tone made him afraid to reject the offer. He sipped his coffee and grinned at her. "Miss, I'd love a piece of pie. If you don't mind, could I have a little more of that coffee to go with it?"

He slid his chair back and began rising to fetch the coffee himself.

"Oh, sit down!" she scolded, grabbing a leather swatch off the table. "Since I'm already up, I might as well get it."

Longarm eased back down in his chair. "Yes, ma'am." He figured Mary Lou, who probably didn't run into strangers all that often, wasn't mad, just shy, and to scold and grumble was her way of communicating without betraying her vulnerability. He'd known many country folk with similar dispositions.

"Yes, ma'am."

"And don't call me ma'am," she scolded again as she filled his coffee cup with the piping-hot, tar-black brew. "I'm only nineteen, so I won't answer to ma'am. Call me Mary Lou if you've a mind to call me anything."

"Thank you kindly, Mary Lou."

As the girl returned the coffeepot to the range, he winced in anticipation of another rebuke. When none came, and he could only hear her over there, whipping the cream and cutting the pie, he added another jigger of bourbon to his coffee and sat there, trying to think of some conversational topic that might not piss her off.

When she'd served him and herself each a piece of pie,

he was mildly surprised to see her add bourbon to her own coffee. He thought maybe the bourbon would loosen her up a little and they might have a conversation. So after she'd had a few sips and had taken a couple bites of the pie—which wasn't too bad in spite of the burnt crust and slightly dry and overly sugary apricot filling—he made a few attempts at small talk.

When his observations about the weather and the heat of the midsummer—and "Gosh, I bet it gets mighty quiet out here!"—were all met with one-word answers or indecipherable murmurs, her eyes never meeting his, he threw back the last of his coffee and bourbon, wiped his mouth with a napkin, and rose from the table.

He wished like hell he'd left the girl to fend for herself. Thanking her for the pie as graciously as possible, he excused himself from the table, slipped out the door, and strode off in search of his horse.

"Damn you, Jim," he muttered as he walked the trail between the chalky buttes. "Why didn't you tell me your daughter was part she-griz with the manners of a coyote?"

The horse hadn't gone far from where he'd dropped its reins, but Longarm took his time returning to the ranch yard, unsaddling the mount, graining, watering, and currying it. Finally, he turned it into the corral with Friendly's own three saddle ponies. By the time he'd strolled around the buildings, making sure no one was stealing up on the place, and had turned his hat toward the cabin, the sun was angling over the western mountains, and meadowlarks sang dolefully from the corral posts and the willows lining the creek.

He was thirty feet from the cabin when he stopped suddenly and sniffed the air. The smoke from the cabin's chimney pipe smelled like steak.

The cabin door latch clicked, and the timber door swung open. Mary Lou stepped out, a broom in one hand, a tin dustpan in the other. As she moved toward a barrel left of the front door, she turned her head toward Longarm and stopped suddenly. Her face coloring, she continued over to the barrel, into which she emptied the dustpan.

As she turned back to the open door, she glanced once more at Longarm staring at her from the ranch yard. He ran his eyes quickly up and down her slender, nicely curved figure, noting with an involuntary male pang of lust that she'd changed into a frilly, low-cut blouse that left her shoulders bare and accentuated her round breasts, and that she'd combed out her hair and secured it neatly in a rich French braid, leaving little curlicues to hang about her cheeks.

The girl lowered her gaze once more, tan cheeks still flushed, and walked back inside the cabin, leaving the door hanging wide behind her.

Longarm stared after her for a couple of seconds. "Well, I'll be damned." Hitching up his pants and gunbelt, he continued walking, frowning, toward the cabin.

Chapter 6

Longarm walked slowly through the door, which Mary Lou
had left open for him. As he closed the door behind him, he
looked at the girl standing at the kitchen range, her back to
him as she poked at the two hefty beefsteaks sizzling and
sputtering in a cast-iron skillet.

He hadn't just been seeing a mirage created by the failing
evening light outside. She had indeed changed out of her
shapeless brown print dress into the low-cut blouse and a
long, purple skirt, obviously homespun but vaguely Spanish-
looking with small red stars sewn into the vertical pleats.
Around the girl's neck was a plain black choker. Her hair
shone as if she'd just combed it, and arranged it neatly in a
rich, black bun behind her head. Her delicate shoulders were
revealed by the low-cut blouse, inviting a man's hands.

She glanced at Longarm, who hadn't yet latched the door,
but stood holding the door's porcelain knob, not sure if he
should mention Mary Lou's change of clothes or keep his
mouth shut and act like nothing had happened.

Did she always dress for dinner out here in the country, or
had she changed for *him*?

She glanced at him over her bare shoulder, and the blush
shone in her right cheek, though her eyes were cold as ever.
"Pa had some steak aging in the cellar, so I figured I might as

well fry it up. Potatoes and biscuits are in the oven, but don't expect anything fancy. This ain't no Denver restaurant, and I ain't no French cook."

Longarm closed the door and doffed his hat. "Maybe not, but that sure is a nice getup, Mary Lou."

Without turning toward him, and still poking and prodding the steak, though it seemed to be frying just fine on its own, she jerked her shoulders. "What—these old rags? Sit down and have a drink if you've a mind. I'll have this grub on the table shortly."

"Smells good," Longarm said with a grin, scrutinizing the girl's round ass behind her skirt as he tossed his hat on the rack by the door. He plucked a cheroot from his shirt pocket as he slid a chair out with his boot, and sat down at the table.

Miss Friendly might have changed clothes, but she hadn't changed personalities, Longarm discovered as, while sipping his bourbon and smoking his cheroot, he made several more futile attempts at polite conversation. He satisfied himself with watching her move around the kitchen, breasts swaying behind the low-cut cotton blouse as she set the table without looking at him, her round butt and curved hips jerking nicely behind the skirt as she stirred gravy at the range with a fork.

He had to remind himself a couple of times that while no one could blame a man for enjoying a pretty figure from a distance, she was not to be messed with. He was here to protect the girl, whether or not she needed protecting. Besides, she was the daughter of a friend, and Jim had already warned the federal deputy off his sullen, sensuous, half-breed offspring.

Neither said anything as she put the food on the table—a small bowl containing the baked potatoes, thick gravy peppered with specks of burned grease, some canned green beans that were almost hot, and the two steaks.

"Help yourself," Mary Lou said, splashing bourbon into her coffee cup. She glanced at him, her pretty, hazel eyes turning foxy. "Unless you pray before you eat, Deputy Long."

"If I can call you Mary Lou, you can call me Custis." Longarm plopped an overdone steak onto his plate. "And no, I'm not given to formalities, Christian or otherwise."

That was the first time he'd seen her smile, though the smile was fleeting—a mere sparkle in her right eye as she narrowed both eyes and briefly lifted her mouth corners. She quickly turned her head away to pluck the other steak onto her plate, then a potato, which she cut open and smothered with gravy.

He didn't bother to chat over supper, except to compliment Mary Lou on the vittles. She did not respond. He did, however, catch her glancing at him occasionally, turning away quickly when his eyes moved toward her.

This was one strange albeit beautiful coyote. She'd obviously dressed up to exhibit her wares—and they were some delectable wares—but she couldn't hold a conversation for shit. . . .

After supper, which concluded with another slice of pie and whipped cream, Longarm offered to help his taciturn hostess clean up. Receiving the expected grunt and chuff, he donned his hat, picked up his rifle, and excused himself, telling Mary Lou he was going to stroll about the buttes, take some air, smoke a cigar, and make sure the dwarf hadn't sent more curly wolves to break more glass and bloody the ranch yard.

Shouldering the rifle, his free hand in his vest pocket, Longarm checked on the horses, then walked out behind the barn to the creek murmuring in the hushed, early evening silence. The land was dark, but the sky remained emerald-green, adorned with mare's-tail clouds brushed with pink.

When he'd walked a half mile east along the creek, then retraced his footsteps and continued for another half mile beyond where he'd started, he circled the ranch yard, enjoying the cool, dry air and the silence interrupted only by the coo of night birds and the intermittent yammering of a distant coyote.

Moving through a fold in the buttes, he spied a well-worn path to the top of one directly behind the cabin. He took the trail, his boots puffing the thick, chalky dust, then sat down at the top and to finish his cigar.

Peering out over the darkening buttes shouldering off to the northwest, the last sunlight gilding a distant creek peeking out between two rimrocks, he speculated about the dwarf and the girl he'd been assigned to fetch from Coyote Flats just across the Wyoming–Dakota border.

Had the dwarf, apparently knowing she was chirping about his bad behavior concerning the crooked mayor, sent curly wolves her way? If Longarm remembered correctly, there were plenty of isolated coulees in that remote country around Coyote Flats on a long curve of Crow Creek snaking south from the Black Hills. Plenty of places in which to dump the body of a talkative showgirl . . .

Longarm hoped he'd find Miss Rogers and that she'd prattle on to the judge. If not, his friend Jim Friendly would have to release the dwarf, which would no doubt make Jim's job of maintaining peace in Chugwater all the more complicated, if not downright impossible.

"Wishin' on a star?"

The girl's voice made Longarm whip his head around, his heart pounding. She was cresting the butte behind him, a blurry figure in the late light, her skirt swishing about her legs. She was barefoot, her bare feet chalky with dust. In her right hand she held her father's bourbon bottle by the neck.

Longarm was chagrined and peeved at himself for letting the girl sneak up on him, barefoot or not. "You shouldn't walk up on a man with a rifle, Miss Mary Lou. Without announcing yourself, I mean."

She only chuckled huskily and moved up beside him. She held the bottle toward him. He looked up at her, his eyes trailing across the round breasts rising and falling behind the flimsy blouse, to her hair, which she'd taken out of the French braid to let hang down across her slender, olive shoulders.

As she looked down at him, a knowing smile on her full lips, her hair, which she'd removed from the braid, winged down both sides of her face. One hazel eye caught a ray of vagrant light, and glistened.

Some of her shyness was gone.

"Obliged," he growled, lowering the rifle and taking the bottle in his right hand. He popped the cork and took a sip, then handed it back up to her.

She didn't take it back, but sat on a rock about two feet below him and right. She stretched her long legs down the hill but angled toward him, and crossed her bare feet. The skirt had come up to reveal nearly all of one sleek shin.

She placed her hands in her lap and looked away. Longarm looked at her profile, then found his eyes dropping involuntarily to her deep cleavage, which he had a good view of from this angle. Her breasts swelled up from the cotton blouse deliciously, and he felt the old fist of lust wrap its fingers around his heart.

He wished she hadn't come out here. He'd vowed long ago that, while he indeed fancied himself a ladies' man and frolicked whenever he could, he rarely slept with whores, and never with married women or the daughters of men he knew personally. The first he simply found unnecessary most of the time. Sleeping with married women or daughters, he'd wisely concluded, could lead to an early grave. (He wasn't friends with Cynthia Larimer's father nor her famous uncle, the general.)

And since his job was already risky, why add two more hazards?

An uncomfortable silence stretched to a good ten minutes. Finally, he took another sip from the bottle, then gave it back to Mary Lou. He hoped she'd take the bottle and leave. She took a liberal sip of the bourbon, wiped her mouth with the back of her hand, corked the bottle, then turned to him suddenly—the first time she'd looked at him since sitting down.

"Don't you like girls?"

Longarm scowled. "Huh?"

"I changed out of that dowdy ole dress just for you and you haven't even tried to kiss me."

"Look, you're a pretty girl. But your father is trusting me to protect you, not molest you! Besides, I thought you were shy."

53

She got down off her rock and knelt beside Longarm, dug her right hand into his thigh. "A girl don't get much . . . fun, if you know what I mean . . . livin' out here with just her pa. Aside from galloping bareback, that is . . ."

She threw her hair back, then reached up and slid the right arm band of her blouse down her arm, revealing all but the tip of her right breast. When she started on the left band, Longarm threw his hands up, palms out. "Hold on now, young lady! You're Jim Friendly's daughter, damnit, and I have principles!"

"Oh, don't get your long handles in a twist! I'm not askin' you to steal the horses or run off with Pa's buried gold. I'm just askin' for a good old roll in the hay!"

Longarm was about to respond, but his throat closed up when he looked down and saw that her blouse, pulled low enough to reveal nearly all of her well-shaped breasts, was hanging by her nipples.

She gave him a wolfish smile, licked her upper lip, then used her right index finger to give the blouse a little jerk. It slipped off the nipples and fell to her waist.

She gave him a minute to war with himself. "What're your principles telling you now?"

Longarm's heart was fluttering. He set the rifle down. "Ah, Christ . . ."

"I had a feelin' that's what they were sayin'."

He pushed onto his knees, took her in his arms, and kissed her hungrily. To his sudden way of thinking, it was Jim's own fault if he didn't know what a randy mink his daughter was. No man could be expected to resist such a hellcat. This was, in fact, tantamount to male rape.

Not his fault at all . . .

In seconds, he had her back on the soft grass of the butte slope, and she was kissing him hungrily while unbuckling his cartridge belt, groaning and nibbling his lips. When she was unable to free the belt hook from the tongue, he pulled away from her, causing her to groan louder, then removed the belt from around his waist and tossed it over a sage clump.

Then, while she lay back in the thick grass, pulling her skirt up and arranging her hair behind her, he kicked his boots off and shucked out of his clothes as fast as he ever had, then dropped to his knees and looked down at her.

She lay spread out before him like a smorgasbord of earthly delights, blouse around her waist, skirt hiked up around her hips. Obviously, she hadn't been wearing a stitch of underwear. Her legs were spread, bent, and raised toes curled, and she reached toward him with her hands, twittling her fingers like a girl yearning to open her birthday present. . . .

"Hurry!" she said.

Longarm knelt there, staring down at her, his mind racing while his loins throbbed. It wasn't too late to turn off this primrose path fraught with thorns.

She must have read his mind. Forming a devilish smile in the semidarkness beneath him, her face an olive oval in the rich, black halo of her hair, she reached down and closed her right hand around his jutting cock.

Her warm hand sent shock waves down his spine.

As she pumped him, laughing and flapping her legs like wings and lifting her head to watch her hand knead him until he was hard as an ax handle, she made up his mind for him.

He thrust his hips forward, impaling her. She threw her head back and yowled as she dug her heels into his back. He hammered away at her for only a couple of minutes before he exploded inside her, rising onto his toes and leaning forward on his outstretched arms as his seed spurted deep within her, his hips jerking spasmodically, his toes digging holes in the bluff.

"*Oh, God! Oh, God!*" she howled, clutching her heels with her hands to spread her legs as wide as she could, the tendons standing out in her neck.

He held her there for a long time after they'd both stopped coming. He kept his face within inches of hers, staring down at her.

Her fingers digging into his biceps, she stared back at him coldly, breathing hard. Her cold, penetrating gaze held

55

him, mesmerized him, and he never totally lost his erection. When his shaft was hard once more, he began thrusting again with his hips.

"Uh," she grunted, frowning and wiggling around beneath him, dropping her legs to the ground. She placed her hands on his broad chest, and pushed. "I wanna be on top this time!"

Without leaving her, he rolled onto his back, and she rolled on top of him, straddling him. The movement made him even harder.

He kneaded her breasts and pinched her nipples as she rose up and down on her haunches, lowering her head until her hair hid her face. The thick black tresses bounced across his chest as her thrusts quickened and deepened, and she was fairly screaming as, digging her fingernails into his shoulders, she galloped the proverbial old warhorse across the pasture and into the barn.

They lay back against the butte, sweaty and spent and staring speechlessly up at the stars. Guilt racked Longarm as he thought of Jim Friendly, who'd trusted Longarm with his daughter's honor.

The racking didn't last long, however. With her expert fingers and lips, Mary Lou convinced him it would be fun to walk back down to the cabin stuck together like dogs.

What the hell? The damage was done.

Longarm pushed himself to his feet with Mary Lou impaled on his cock, her heels locked behind his back, hands around his neck.

The walk down the bluff, with the warm chalky dust under his feet and all the natural jostling enhanced by Mary Lou's bouncing, made them both come again.

They came once more as he did her up against the barn wall before they both half crawled to the cabin and passed out on her bunk like drunken pirates.

Chapter 7

A horse whinnied.

Longarm lifted his head from the pillow with a jerk, and looked around the dim cabin. The horse whinnied again, and boots thumped on the porch. The latch was tripped with a click, and as the door swung open, the lawman whipped his sleep-thick head around for his gun, blinking his eyes to clear his vision.

The revolver was nowhere in sight.

Remembering he'd left the firearm and all his clothes on the bluff where he and Mary Lou had frolicked under the stars, he turned toward the front of the cabin. Mary Lou appeared around the door, her arms heaped with his and her clothes, his gunbelt draped over her right shoulder.

She was a striking figure, standing there in the open doorway, his snuff-brown Stetson on her head, one of his cigars protruding from between her lips, and his overlarge boots reaching up nearly to her knees. Otherwise, she wore only a long, gray shirt, which hung down to just below her snatch.

Chomping down on the lit cigar, she squinted against the smoke, gave the door a kick, and strode past the table and dumped the load of clothes on the floor beside the cot.

"Best get your duds on and hightail it," she said in her customary growl, removing the cigar from her mouth with one hand as she draped his gunbelt over a chair back with the other. "Your stage'll be pullin' out in one hour, and Pa can't hold it forever."

"Christ!" Longarm grunted, pressing his fingertips to his forehead, wincing against the guilt pangs. "It wasn't a nightmare?"

Staring down at him, puffing his cigar, Mary Lou scowled. "Nightmare?"

He kicked the single quilt off his naked frame and dropped his feet to the floor. "I fucked my good friend's daughter . . . and here when he trusted me . . ."

"I wouldn't feel so bad," Mary Lou said, cocking one foot and tapping ashes onto the floor. "I had a pretty good hand in it my ownself. And stronger men have succumbed to my charms. I'd give you something else to feel guilty about," she said, licking her lips, "but if you miss that stage, Pa's liable to get suspicious."

Longarm looked at her as she tossed his hat onto the chair back and shook out her hair, breasts pushing out from behind the threadbare shirt, nipples resembling small buttons.

"You're a caution, Mary Lou."

Offering a rare grin, she turned and, his boots scraping the floorboards beneath her small feet, shuffled over to the ticking range in which she must've laid a fire before she'd retrieved their duds. "Does that mean you'll stop and see me again sometime?"

"Don't think my conscience could take it."

"Spoilsport," she said as she opened the range door and tossed another log into the firebox.

Longarm gave himself a whore's bath with water Mary Lou provided, then slugged a cup of coffee and downed a couple of egg biscuits before bidding the bewitching beauty good-bye. She held him on the porch for nearly a full minute, kissing him hungrily as she rose up on her bare toes, gripping his coat lapels in her fists.

Releasing him, she extended another smile, which caused his heart to throb and gave him dangerous second thoughts about leaving. "Good-bye, Custis. If I never see you again, just know you made my year."

He drew her to him again, planted one tender kiss on her lips and another on her forehead. He stepped back, pinched his hat brim to her, then turned, grabbed his reins from the hitch rack, and swung onto the claybank. Seconds later, he galloped out of the yard, heading southwest toward Chugwater as the morning birds sang in the cottonwoods.

Chugwater was still half-asleep as Longarm cantered into town twenty minutes later, wood smoke hovering in blue clouds between the false fronts of Main Street. The Dwarf House was silent except for a whore in pantaloons and a pink kimono trimming her toenails on the front steps while a pimply-faced young man in blue coveralls ran a strainer through a horse trough, the water tinkling clearly in the early quiet.

Longarm hadn't gotten directions to the stage depot, but it wasn't hard to find, since the dusty red and yellow Concord was sitting in the otherwise empty street before it. Jim Friendly stood at the rear of the stage, hands in his pockets as he stared toward Longarm, nibbling his mustache. A woman in a poke bonnet had her head out the right-side window, staring after Longarm as well, an impatient set to her dull, doughy features.

The sheriff's badge shone in the foggy gray dawn, and his oiled Remington jutted from the holster on his right hip.

"How was your night? Any trouble?" Friendly asked as Longarm hit the ground jogging.

"Quiet as a boneyard out there." Longarm avoided eye contact with the man as he tossed the reins to him, and made for the coach door. "My possibles on board?"

"They're in the rear boot," Friendly said as he turned and walked up to the front of the stage. "Custis, say hidy to Ben Pensiero, the jahoo, and his sidekick, Jim Anderson. They're two good pards of mine and if anyone can get you to Douglas in one piece, it's them. I done told 'em what you're up to, and they promised not to dally at the relay stations."

"Hidy, fellers," Longarm said, grinning up at the driver, a wizened, sunburned man with Italian-dark eyes and mustache, and the rangy, blue-eyed gent cradling a double-barreled shotgun in his arms, a red polka-dot neckerchief billowing over his chest, his blond hair knife-cut in a straight line across his forehead.

Anderson didn't say anything, but the driver sitting to his left nodded cordially. "We'll make your trip as fast and comfortable as possible, Deputy. Hop aboard and we'll lift some dust."

"Yes, please hop aboard, sir," said the middle-aged woman still poking her blond head out the window. "We have to make the church picnic in Douglas at six o'clock this evening, and if we don't get moving soon, I'll just have a *fit*! The reason I never take the *train* is the *delays*!"

"Our apologies, Mrs. Hartman!" Tipping his hat to the biddy and opening the stage door, Jim Friendly turned to Longarm. "I got a telegram back from the Coyotes Flats town constable. He said he was going to keep a close eye on the witness, and if she tried to leave town, he'd hold her. Oh, that reminds me—here's the subpoena all filled out and signed by the judge."

Halfway into the stage, Longarm turned and grabbed the small manila envelope from Friendly. "Don't worry, Jim."

Longarm crabbed past the blond woman and the eldery, well-dressed gent sitting beside her, as well as a little girl sitting across from Mrs. Hartman, and sank into the seat on the far side of the stage, facing the rear. Friendly closed the door and yelled up to the driver, "All set, Ben!"

Longarm felt the stage quiver as the driver and shotgun messenger adjusted themselves in the driver's box. There was a wooden bark as the brake was released. The crack of the blacksnake echoed like a rifle shot in the quiet morning air. As the driver hoorawed the horses and the three other passengers grabbed the hand straps for support, Friendly ran up to Longarm's window, looking harried. "Remember," the sheriff said as the stage jerked forward, "you gotta have the girl here for a Friday hearing, or I gotta release the dwarf! Four days, Custis!"

Friendly turned to stare after the stage rumbling and clattering northward along the main drag. The suited sheriff grew smaller behind it as he cupped his hands around his mouth. "So whatever you do—*don't dally!*"

A second later, Friendly disappeared behind the dust cloud trailing the stage. Seconds after that, the scraggly edges of Chugwater were replaced by rolling prairie and distant rimrocks, the sunrise blossoming behind even more distant rimrocks in the east.

"So, you're a U.S. marshal, huh?"

Longarm turned to see the little girl to his left looking at him from behind her silver-framed spectacles. She was a round-faced child with a bullet-crowned hat with a silk band from which a pink daisy protruded. She wore a simple brown traveling dress that reached to just below her knees, and high, black socks rose up from her button shoes. The shoes didn't quite reach the stage floor. She was dimple-cheeked cute, with tan, boyish features untempered by her white shirt and bow tie.

Longarm glanced at the blond woman—a beefy lady with jowls—and her husband, who wore muttonchops and a preacher's collar too tight for his florid neck. They both regarded him with mild reproof, obviously piqued that he'd delayed their travel. He wished Friendly hadn't mentioned his assignment in front of Longarm's fellow passengers, but neither the little girl nor the couple were likely a threat to his mission.

He turned back to the little girl staring up at him with wide-eyed curiosity.

"That's right, little lady." He pinched his hat brim to her and offered one of his disarming smiles. "Custis Long is my handle, but you can call me Longarm."

The girl giggled, keeping her eyes on him. "Longarm? What kind of silly name is that?"

Longarm felt his face warm, and he glanced self-consciously at the other two traveling companions, whose expressions had not changed.

"That's my nickname," he told the girl, trying not to sound defensive. "You know—the long arm of the law, and such."

"Oh, I see." She gave the seat a couple of idle kicks. "You must be really good, huh?"

"I do my best."

"Wanna play cards?" She reached into a pocket of her wool jacket and showed him a deck of playing cards.

Longarm glanced at the couple sitting across from the girl. "I suspect your folks wouldn't approve of cardplayin', miss."

The girl glanced at the couple, then shuttled her gaze back to Longarm. "Oh, they're not my folks. In fact, aside from Aunt Gert, I don't have any family except an uncle in Yuma Penitentiary. And Aunt Gertie's the one who taught me to play poker—five different games—in the first place!"

Before Longarm could respond, the blond woman clucked and dipped her chin at the child. "Young lady, card-playing is an undesirable activity."

"It is?" the girl said.

"It certainly is," said the preacher, his turkey neck spilling over his collar as he mirrored his wife's admonishing chin dip. His shaggy brows formed an inverted, gray-brown V above the bridge of his nose.

The girl turned to Longarm, lower jaw hanging as though she'd just been told there's no Santa Claus. "It *is*? But Aunt Gertie's been playing cards over to the Happy Gal for as long as I've been alive!"

"Pshaw!" Longarm said, glancing at the righteous pair shuffling scowls between him and the girl. "Deal 'em out, little gal! What're we playing for—toothpicks or lucifers?"

"How 'bout nickels? I'm on my way back home from Uncle Ned's funeral in Julesburg"—she lifted her right arm, jingling a coin sack strapped somewhere up her sleeve—"and his will left me flush as Jesse James!"

The girl dealt the cards, her small, tan, slightly soiled

hands working the deck like an experienced mechanic. Just seeing her shuffle and deal so slickly made it obvious that Aunt Gertie had been teaching the girl the tricks of the aunt's "undesirable" trade. So when Longarm, not playing to his full potential, was out two dollars and fifty cents after the first hour of play—and that was even throwing in a little red dog for variety—he was certain the tyke wasn't being raised right at all.

As any other self-respecting male would have done in a similar situation, Longarm rolled up his sleeves and got serious.

And by the second water stop, he was out three twenty-five!

"Dang, you little devil!" Longarm laughed as the stage creaked to a jerky stop, raising the girl's left hand to check her sleeves for spare cards. "You're a sharpie if I ever seen one!"

The girl, whose name Longarm had learned was Lida Anne Leonard, chuckled as she brushed the pot off the seat between her and Longarm and into her cupped right hand. She dropped the coins with a flourish into her brimming deerskin pouch, and brushed her hands together.

"And you encourage her!" railed the preacher's wife as her husband assisted her out the coach's open door, shaking his head at Longarm as though at an acolyte who'd let his candles burn out.

As Longarm followed Lida Anne out of the stage, the driver announced that, as the horses had to be unhitched and led to a creek a good fifty yards off the trail, they'd be stopped for a good half hour. While Lida Anne and the others tended nature off in the boulders, Longarm stole a quick drink from the Maryland rye bottle secured in his war bag. Fortified, and having decided his stiff legs needed stretching, he set his hat for the creek down a rocky hill and on the other side of a thick grove of dusty cottonwoods.

Fifteen minutes later, when he'd had a short walk and a cool drink from the creek, he walked halfway back up the rocky hill to the stage, then stopped in the shade of a cottonwood to light a cigar. He'd taken a couple of puffs when he heard footsteps to his left, and turned to see the girl meandering around the butte shoulder.

She was heading toward him, absently shuffling the card deck in her hands.

"Sorry, Lida Anne," Longarm said, studying his cigar's coal and blowing smoke through his nostrils. "You done fleeced me clean of pocket jingle."

"Longarm?"

"Miss?"

"It must be pretty exciting being a lawman, huh?"

"It beats poker."

"Do you have to shoot a lot of bad guys?"

"Oh, some."

Lida Anne widened her eyes as she stared up at Longarm, and raised her voice an octave or two. "Ever have to pistol-whip 'em like in the stories of Mr. Buntline?"

Longarm chuckled as he stuck his fingers in his vest pockets and looked off across the creek, drawing on the cigar in his teeth. "Pistol-whippin' often comes in handy, Lida Anne—especially when you're dealin' with the really *bad* element!"

Longarm chuckled again.

"Mr. Longarm?"

"Mmm-hmm?"

"Why is that man standing on that rock up there?"

Longarm jerked his gaze to the top of the boulder. A yellow-haired, bespectacled man in a shabby suit with checked pants and a battered bowler hat stood atop the rock, extending a cocked revolver, sighting down the barrel at Longarm.

Clawing for his .44, Longarm threw himself and the girl back toward the base of the boulder. "Get down, Lida Anne!"

Above, the revolver popped, blowing up a clod of sand and weeds from Longarm's right boot print. Looking up from this angle, Longarm couldn't see much of the shooter but his gun and right wrist, angling down steeply as the dry-gulcher tried to draw a bead on the lawman.

The gun belched smoke, blowing up another sand clod two feet beyond Longarm. The pistol popped again.

"Hunker low, Lida Anne!" Longarm yelled to the girl cowering in the shade at the base of the rock.

Thumbing back his Colt's hammer, he stepped out from the boulder and raised the revolver nearly straight up, slitting one eye.

The dry-gulcher's spectacles glinted in the sunlight as he turned his head toward Longarm, his lower jaw sagging with surprise. As he readjusted his aim, Longarm drilled the man twice through the brisket.

The bushwhacker screamed and dropped his pistol as he clutched his chest with both hands. He sagged to his knees, then tumbled over the side of the boulder. Longarm bolted forward to cover Lida Anne with his own body as the bushwhacker turned a somersault in the air behind him, and hit the ground with a thud and a loud fart.

Dust wafted around the man's inert body, checked pants and shabby brown coat glowing in the crisp sunlight, the man's cracked glasses hanging askew. His bowler rolled off with the breeze.

"Wow!" Lida Anne exclaimed as, hunkered down at the base of the boulder, she lowered her arms from her head to stare wide-eyed at the dead dry-gulcher. "Two shots right through the heart!"

"Stay here, Lida Anne!" Longarm ordered the girl as he stepped out again from the boulder, swinging his pistol around as he looked for more bushwhackers.

He circled the scarp twice, spying no one near or far, but hearing the preacher and the preacher's wife caterwauling around the stage. Yelling for the couple to stay where they were, Longarm jogged down to the river, where he spied a single horse tethered a good seventy yards downstream, in cottonwoods lining the opposite bank.

When he made his way back to the scarp, Reverend and Mrs. Hartman, and the stage driver, Ben Pensiero, had gathered around the dead man. The driver was hunkered down over the man, running a hand nervously across his bearded chin.

"Are you sure he's dead?" asked the preacher's wife, her voice trilling fearfully as she bunched her black skirts in her fists.

"Deader'n a doornail!" exclaimed Lida Anne, looking at Longarm.

"Young lady, that's awful talk!" Mrs. Hartman scolded Lida Anne. "You run back to the stage, and I'll be along in a minute to read you some Bible verses!"

Ignoring the woman, Lida Anne ran two steps forward, then wheeled and aimed her imaginary pistol at the top of the scarp. "Pow! Pow! That's how he done it. Two shots right through the brisket." She clutched her chest with both hands and, batting her eyes and slackening her cheek muscles as though on her way out of this world, she dropped to her knees and rolled forward, grinding her forehead into the dirt.

"I apologize for the young lady's theatrics, ma'am," Longarm said to the preacher's wife. "But that *is* pretty much how it happened."

Chapter 8

"What happened, Deputy?" the driver asked, straightening as he turned to Longarm, sweat glistening through the dust on his sallow, bearded cheeks. "And who is this hombre anyway?"

Longarm opened his mouth to speak, but stopped when the man he'd thought was dead jerked suddenly, and coughed.

"He's alive!" exclaimeed the preacher, leaping straight back and grabbing his wife's arm.

The dry-gulcher stretched his lips back from his teeth and wheezed, blood frothing on his lips. Longarm's bullets had taken him through both lungs.

The federal lawman motioned for everyone to back away, then jerked his tweed trousers up his thighs and hunkered down beside the mortally wounded bushwhacker, tossing the man's glasses away and giving his collar a tug. "Who the hell are you, old son, and why were you trying to shoot me from atop that rock?"

Longarm didn't expect much of an answer. Even near death, professional regulators were a taciturn lot, clinging to the code that kept their employers' dirty secrets. So the lawman was surprised when the man lifted his head and grabbed Longarm's coat lapel.

Scowling and spitting blood from his lips, he said, "The albino . . . said it'd be simple as apple pie. Just wait for the damn stage to stop for water . . . plug you a coupla times . . . an' hightail it . . . and all my gambling debts—"

The man winced as pain choked him.

"Would be forgiven," Longarm finished for him. Glancing at the stage driver scowling down with both fists on his hips, Longarm said, "The dwarf in Chugwater have an albino workin' for him?"

The driver nodded, chuckling. "J. Mortimer St. Paul, his lawyer."

The bushwhacker lowered his head to the ground, sobbing. "Ah, shit, I ain't no killer. I'm just a fucking gambler, and look at me now, lying here in front of all of you . . . *dyin'*!"

"What's your name?"

The man didn't answer for a time, and Longarm thought he was dead. Then the man croaked almost inaudibly, "Howard." He swallowed and coughed more blood. "Melvin Howard from Ashwater, Kentucky. And . . . I wish I never laid eyes on *Chugwater, Wymoming*! Oh, why didn't I keep on to Billings *like I planned*?"

Longarm was vaguely aware of the preacher and his wife ushering Lida Anne back toward the stage, the girl complaining while Mrs. Hartman clucked and cajoled.

"How'd you know where the stage was gonna stop for water?" Such information was easily acquired, but someone from the stage line might have been in cahoots with the poor sot as well.

Longarm had barely finished the question before the man's body relaxed and his eyes went glassy. His chest fell still.

Longarm cursed and straightened as the driver, Pensiero, said, "Wonder where in the hell he's goin'."

Longarm looked at the sun-battered jahoo, then followed the man's puzzled gaze down the rocky, brush-stippled slope to the cottonwoods lining the creek. On the other side of the stream, the blond shotgun rider, Jim Anderson, was scrambling up the far hill, moving as though fleeing a wildfire, pulling at the weed tufts to assist his ascent toward the chalky knobs above.

Anderson paused halfway up the hill to glance over his right shoulder, then wheeled forward and continued moving up the grade as though the hounds of hell were nipping at his heels.

Longarm fished a cold, half-smoked cigar from his pocket, and stuck it in his mouth. Staring after the fleeing shotgun rider, he scraped a match to life on his holster, touched the flame to his cigar. He dropped the match and stepped on it, blowing smoke through his nose.

"I gotta feelin' I know how poor ole Howard knew where to camp out here." Longarm snorted as the shotgun rider scrambled around a chalky knob protruding from the hillside, slipping, falling, and scrambling back to his feet, clawing at the weeds for purchase. "That blond-headed nut must've figured Howard was tellin' deathbed tales."

"Damn," Pensiero said, scratching his gaunt, leathery cheek as he stared after Anderson. "I thought he'd been acting a might on edge of late. Figured it was just his wife was on the rag."

Longarm cocked a brow at the driver. "If you're in cahoots with him and the gent growing colder at our ankles, Ben, tell me now so we can have it out and over with. I'd be mighty sore if one of the other passengers caught a pill meant for me later on down the trail."

The driver was still staring after his younger, blond-headed partner, who had now dropped down the other side of the butte he'd been climbing. "I make more money than I can spend on whiskey and women workin' for the stage line . . . without gettin' the clap or a boggy liver, that is." He turned a sidelong glance to Longarm, lifting one mouth corner. "Why would I need to start drillin' badge-toters?"

Longarm left the double-crossing shotgun rider to the rattle-snakes and grizzly bears, which would no doubt claim him if renegade Cheyenne or Sioux didn't get to him first, and secured the bushwhacker, Melvin Howard of Ashwater, Kentucky, to the top of the stage, wrapped in his own saddle blanket.

When Longarm had retrieved and tied the man's horse to the rear saddle boot, he climbed atop the stage to ride shotgun for Pensiero. The jahoo released the brake, snugged his hat brim low, raised his neckerchief over his nose, shook the ribbons over the six-hitch's backs, and the stage lunged off once more for Douglas, Wyoming Territory, and Coyote Flats just over the line in Dakota.

In spite of the dust and hard wooden seat beneath his ass, Longarm was glad to be away from Lida Anne, whose obsession for poker—not to mention her prowess—had grown right tiresome. He'd also grown tired of the preacher and the preacher's wife, whom, when the driver walked the horses up hills, Longarm could hear reading to the poor girl Bible verses related to "false gods" and "idle pursuits."

There were three more relay stations and one town between Chugwater and Douglas. The Hartmans got off at Douglas, doubtless to Lida Anne's delight, and two drummers and a stockman in a brushed gray suit and high-crowned cream Stetson climbed aboard. They were on the stage when the Concord rolled into Coyote Flats just after dark the next night, and pulled up at the stage depot and barn.

The coach's pungent dust cloud caught up to it as Longarm turned to Pensiero. "This is the end of the line for me and my sore ass, Ben. The end for ole Melvin Howard of Ashwater, Kentucky, too, though I'm sure the local law ain't gonna enjoy the paperwork."

"Happens to be the end fer me my ownself," said the jahoo as he wrapped the reins around the brake handle. Two beefy hostlers were striding lazily out from the barn, hacking phlegm and scuffing their boot heels across the hard-packed wagon yard. "A new driver and messenger'll take over in the mornin', pull this crate the rest of the way to Fort Pierre. God-fer-fuckin'-saken country, that. Forget the whiskey. You can't even find a decent cup of coffee in that country!"

"Yeah," Longarm grumbled, looking around the motley collection of shacks to the north and south as he stowed the shotgun under the seat. "This here looks like the Promised Land, sure 'nuff."

In the dark, he couldn't see much of Coyote Flats on Crow Creek, but having been through here before on his way to Deadwood, he knew there wasn't much to the place but a few rickety shacks on either side of the block-long main drag abutted in the west by a shallow, muddy stream, with sage flats rolling up to bald, craggy rimrocks in the west and east.

The town had started out as a hide-hunters' and wolfers' camp, with stranded argonauts and their broken-down wagons, tents, and screaming kids camped along the edges. It hadn't changed much since then, except for the pioneers having moved on, leaving a dozen or so derelict prairie schooners succumbing to the sage and shadbush. Somewhere behind Longarm, a piano clattered out of tune, and either a cat was dying in an alley or a girl was trying to sing in one of the half-dozen saloons.

"No, it ain't much," Pensiero said. "But the Trail Blazer serves cold beer and Miss Gertrude's over yonder offers clean gambling and free women to stage drivers who scrape their boots, take a bath, and shave so's we don't chafe her girls' titties." The old jahoo laughed as he gathered his possibles from under the seat.

"When's the next stage out of here?" Longarm asked him.

"There's a stage through here every two days. I think the one from Deadwood cuts through here every Wednesday or Thursday. I don't pay much attention 'cause I don't jahoo that one—and a good thing too, since it always seems to get held up."

Longarm dropped to the ground, landing flat-footed and hoping he hadn't missed the Deadwood stage, whether it was oft targeted by owlhoots or not. This was Tuesday, and he had to get the dwarf's chippie to Chugwater by Friday at noon. Besides, he'd like to be in Denver for the weekend.

Longarm reached for the stage's door handle, hearing the men grumbling inside about having been fleeced by such a sweet-looking child, and indulged in an inward grin.

Longarm and the driver helped all the passengers get off, including Lida Anne, who was jubilantly shaking her hefty coin purse and grinning like the cat who ate the canary. When all the luggage had been passed around, Longarm crawled back up to the coach's roof and used his barlow knife to cut the ropes lashing Melvin Howard's stiffening corpse from the brass side rails.

He and Pensiero eased the body down to the ground, and deposited it on the depot's front stoop before Longarm gathered his own possibles from the stage boot. Hefting his war bag in his left hand, his rifle in the other, he turned to make his way toward the town constable's office, which the coach had passed on the way into town. God willing, he and the dwarf's darling would be headed back toward Chugwater tomorrow.

"If you notify your boss that he's short one shotgun rider," he called over his shoulder to Pensiero, "I'll send someone over shortly for the carcass."

A girl's voice yelled, "Longarm!"

He turned. Lida Anne stood in the middle of the street behind him, her round glasses reflecting the light shed by a nearby hop house. She held a carpetbag in both hands, swinging it to and fro before her, bouncing it against her knees.

"Follow me over to Aunt Gert's place, if you're lookin' for a place to light." A line of white shone between her spread lips as she threw her head back proudly. "She has the most honest gamblin', the best hooch, and finest-lookin' working girls in the territory!"

The girl canted her head toward the big saloon a block away on the right side of the street, from which the piano-clanging and out-of-tune "singing" emanated. Torches on the stout porch posts cast a broad swath of light as they sent glowing cinders skyward. A dozen horses stood at the hitch racks, hip-shot or hang-headed or swishing their tails with a desultory air.

"Miss Lida Anne, your proficiency at gambling is rivaled by only your facility at thumping the tub. Glad to see the Hartmans didn't corrupt you. But if I were to venture into your aunt's place, I doubt I'd feel well rested in the morning for travel." He winked and ticked his hat brim to her. "I'm obliged for the invitation, and I bid you a fond farewell."

Lida Anne shrugged. "Suit yourself, but if you change your mind . . ."

Longarm started to turn away, stopped, and turned back to face the girl as she began moseying toward the well-lit whorehouse and gambling parlor. "Lida Anne, a word of advice?"

She stopped and looked at him.

"When you're markin' your pasteboards with that little ring that looks so sweet on your right pinkie, you should make sure you don't leave any little shavings hanging off the edges. It's a dead giveaway."

The girl turned sharply to face him, frowning. She stomped one high-button shoe in the dark dust. *"You knew all along?"*

"It took me a while, on account of how you look like butter wouldn't melt in your mouth an' all. When I got past that, I noticed the ragged edges you were leaving on the pasteboards, and your pinky ring."

Longarm gave her a wink, then continued heading toward the jailhouse. Lida Anne muttered angrily behind him as she, in turn, slinked off toward Miss Gertrude's whorehouse and gambling parlor.

The jailhouse was a strange-looking building, and Longarm wouldn't have recognized it on his first pass through town unless a shingle jutting into the street from over the porch roof hadn't read JAILHOUSE in large, black letters painted on white. The original stone block with barred front windows and a stout timbered door had been swallowed up by a log addition above and to the right of the original dwelling, giving the place a makeshift, hodgepodge look.

The barred windows were lit from behind, but after the

reception he'd received at Friendly's professional digs in Chugwater, Longarm decided to knock before entering.

"Come on in!"

Resting his Winchester's barrel on his right shoulder, Longarm tripped the door's steel latch and poked the door open with the rifle's butt. After a quick look around the dank, dark room, Longarm slid his eyes back to the unshaven gent in homespuns and a shabby, overlarge dress coat standing behind the door of one of the jailhouse's three cells. The gent's hair was mussed, and he regarded Longarm with amusement.

"Where's the constable?" the lawman asked.

"Out back with his old lady," said the prisoner. "Who the hell are you?"

Longarm stepped back, and was about to draw the door closed behind him when the pudgy gent yelled, "Hey!"

Longarm pushed the door half open and arched a brow.

"Tell that old son of a bitch to either turn me loose or go out to my place and milk my damn cow, will ya?"

"How 'bout if I just do it?"

The man's face brightened. "Hey, would ya?"

Longarm chuffed as he drew the door closed, then walked around the south side of the building. He could see an orange glow ahead. When he walked around the building's rear corner, he stopped.

About twenty feet behind the building, a large bonfire burned in a broad fire ring, near a washtub and a clothesline from which multicolored clothes hung limp. To one side of the fire, an old woman with long, greasy gray hair sat in a creaky rocker, a wool blanket draping her knees, a calico cat resting sphinxlike on her right thigh.

"Who the hell're you?" asked the gent standing before the bloody antelope carcass hanging from the eaves near Longarm. He backed up several feet and waggled the knife at the lawman, threatening. "Come on—out with it, or I'll skin ye where you stand!"

The old woman threw her head back on her bony shoulders, her mad cackling lifting the hairs on the back of Longarm's neck.

Chapter 9

When the old woman finally stopped cackling, Longarm told the old gent with the bloody skinning knife who he was and what he was doing here in Coyote Flats and that he had a dead man stiffening over at the stage depot. "You the constable?"

The man, slump-shouldered and wearing a black knit cap low on his forehead, winced sheepishly and ran the back of his wrist against his scraggly, blood-speckled goatee. "Yeah, I'm the constable. Ogden Bergie. I'll send the undertaker for the stiff, but the showgirl ain't here."

He turned sulkily back to the antelope and resumed cutting inside the open rib cage. The rope securing the dead beast to the eaves squawked as the carcass twisted and turned under the constable's knife.

Longarm sighed. "I understood you were going to make sure Miss Rogers—if that's the name she's still using—stayed here in Coyote Flats, so I could lasso her easy and take her back to Chugwater to sing for Friendly."

The old woman cackled again.

"Shut up, old woman!" Constable Bergie said as he cut off a hunk of meat and slung it into an apple crate on a wheelbarrow to his left. He stopped and turned to Longarm with an impatient chuff. "I tried to grab her before she left town, but I was too late. She done left and, since I don't have no deputies much less a *regular salary*, I didn't saddle a horse to go traipsing after her."

The old woman cackled louder. "He's spewin' bullshit, Marshal!"

She rocked, grinning through her dentures showing yellow in the firelight, and taking a puff from a long, thin cigar she held between her left thumb and index finger. "He went over to Miss Gertrude's to grab that chippie while she was singin' for the cowpokes, and she pulled a peashooter on him. An itty-bitty derringer!"

The old woman slapped the chair arm and blew smoke through her flared nostrils. "Scared him so bad he peed his pants, turned tail, and ran on home to hide behind my broad ass!"

She kicked her slippered feet and thick, spotted ankles out with glee while the cat twitched its tail with annoyance.

"You're gonna be the one doin' the hidin', old woman!" Constable Bergie shouted, turning the bloody knife on his wife. "If you don't shut your damn trap!"

The woman only shook her head and took another drag off the cigar as Bergie turned to Longarm, his broad face, with one deep-sunk eye slightly lower than the other, slack with chagrin. His tone was sulky. "Fact is, the little bitch did pull a gun on me. . . ."

"That big," added Bergie's wife, holding up her left hand and spreading her thumb and index finger three inches apart.

"*Hers* was a peashooter," said Bergie, shuttling his piqued gaze between the old woman and Longarm, "but the bitch who runs that traveling pay-actors' troupe was packin' a sawed-off gut-shredder! Besides, I don't have jurisdiction over that chippie anyways. Wrong county. And I'm *municipal*!"

Longarm didn't see how that mattered, as lawmen from different jurisdictions helped each other all the time. He let it go, however. Constable Bergie had a point. Longarm was getting paid considerably more than the constable was; thus

Longarm should be the one taking the chances, though he hadn't thought that holding a showgirl so that a federal lawman could slap a subpoena on her was taking *any* chances. That she'd resisted Bergie's professional advances meant she'd decided against singing for Friendly and was going to be considerably harder to toss a long loop around.

Especially if someone had already come gunning for her.

Longarm dropped his war bag and poked his hat brim off his forehead as he regarded Bergie with exasperation. "She's with a traveling show troupe now, you say? When'd she leave?"

"Yesterday," Bergie and the old woman said in unison.

"You know where they're headed?"

"Deadwood."

"How many wagons?"

"Three," said the constable and his wife again at the same time.

Longarm scrunched up his eyebrows. "A day's head start to Deadwood would put them where?"

"Pret' near Owl Creek," the old woman said, cutting off her husband.

"Maggie, goddamnit!" railed Bergie, swinging toward her with his knife in his hand. "Who's the constable here?"

The old woman cackled, wrinkling her nose disgustedly. "You wouldn't see me backin' down to no playactin' *chippie*!"

"All right, all right!" Longarm interrupted. He glared at them until they'd both turned toward him, passably cowed, then asked where he could find a quiet place to get a few hours' sleep. He'd rent a horse from the local livery and set off after the showgirl first thing in the morning.

"Right here," said the old woman, canting her head at the cabin–jailhouse's dark second story. "We have an extry cot upstairs. Clean and bedbug-free. We use it for additional income. Bergie's done told you till you're as sick as I am of hearing it, he don't get paid but pennies and pisswater when he *does* get paid.

"Since you're on Uncle Sam's payroll, you can no doubt

afford a couple dollars, and I'll throw in a free bowl of antelope stew, fresh bread, and stewed tomatoes. An extra fifty cents will get you antelope steak and eggs for breakfast."

Before Longarm could respond, Maggie Bergie struggled up out of her chair—all two hundred and fifty pounds of mostly hips and ass. With a hearty "Come on!" she waddled toward the lighted open doorway right of her husband and framed by two spindly lilac shrubs.

Longarm stared after her as she hauled her massive body through the door. After a moment's consideration, he picked up his saddlebags and, as Bergie went back to work on the antelope carcass, strode after the man's obese wife.

He hadn't arranged for any other accommodations, and the Bergies' place would most likely be quieter than your average Coyote Flats hotel—certainly quieter than Aunt Gertie's place with its clanking piano and keening whores. So he followed the old woman into the house and up a rickety set of stairs to a musty second story where she struggled, breathing so hard Longarm thought she would die of a heart seizure, to light a lamp.

With the smoky hurricane lantern lit, she waddled through the open second story, in which there was a bed and a dresser, to a cot sitting against the north wall, on the other side of a blanket partition.

"It ain't much, but it's clean and we keep a quiet house, so you'll get your rest. And I have a feelin' you're gonna need it if you're goin' after them women."

"Women?"

"The troupe's all women, don't you know. And like ole Bergie said, the leader packs a double-barreled barn-blaster. She's pretty as painted sin but ornery as hell! Same with that Miss Rogers you're all steamed up about!"

Maggie Bergie cackled as she set the lamp on a steamer trunk, then, sticking the cigar in her mouth, made for the steep stairs. "Come on, Deputy, and I'll bowl you up some stew!"

Longarm hadn't eaten since Mary Lou's egg biscuits at breakfast, and he found Maggie Bergie's stew delectable. It slid down his throat, spicy and warm and quelling the hunger pangs he'd only half-consciously been aware of. He found the old woman's conversation about her aches and pains and foul well water tedious, however. After scribbling out some notes for a later report on the men he'd kicked off so far on this assignment, and dropping his spoon in his bowl, he made his way back up the stairs to bed. Maggie Bergie continued grumbling behind him.

He arranged the blanket partition to give him and the Bergies as much privacy as possible in the cramped second-story quarters, with its low-slanting walls and clutter of cold-weather clothes, crates, barrels, and ancient, broken furniture. He took a long pull from his rye, then drew the blanket back from the cot, stretched, scratched his belly as he yawned big, and lay down.

He'd barely felt his head hitting the pillow before he drifted off into a deep sleep, only vaguely interrupted later by the shoe scuffs, floor squawks, and grumbling of the Bergies coming to bed.

He had no idea how much time had passed before his eyes snapped open and he pushed up on his elbows, looking around the solid darkness groggily.

What in the hell was making that squawking noise? It sounded like someone rocking fast in a dilapidated rocker—so fast the floor was shaking.

Beneath the squawks of dry wood, grunts and groans rose, and a man cursed through his teeth. Longarm made a sour expression, as though he'd just downed a jigger of camphor.

It wasn't a rocker. The Bergies were doing the dirty not fifteen feet away.

The image evoked by the sounds was as revolting as the noise, and he turned and buried his face in the pillow, clamping both ends against his ears to drown out the cacophony and clear his mind of the vision. The maneuver helped only a little, so he gutted it out for the five minutes it took the old man to reach a hard-fought climax, grumbling and sputtering like a dying bear, and the old woman to grunt and cluck and berate him with, "Fer chrissakes, Bergie, will you get the hell off'n me now?"

There was a tussle of sheets and a few more squawks of the cot. The old man spat, the old woman sighed loudly, as though she was glad to have made it through a prairie twister with her life. The glassy thud must have been Maggie dropping her dentures in a water glass.

Again, Longarm winced, wishing like hell he'd gone over to Auntie Gert's, for surely there was no commotion there worse than what he'd just endured here.

It turned out that the tooth-grinding din of the old couple's carnal knowledge was just the start of the evening. They fell asleep soon after their lovemaking, so Longarm thought he too would soon be asleep.

He almost was, in fact, until the old man began to snore.

The old woman followed suit, her prolonged honks and yammers resounding even louder than the old man's, the two of them fairly bringing down the house around Longarm's head.

The lawman sat up, took another couple of pulls from his rye bottle, shoved a couple of bullet cartridges into his ears lead-first, buried his head in his pillow, and got a passable night's rest—if "passable" includes being woken every hour or so by a sudden rise in pitch or volume of one or the other of the old couple's snores.

Not only that, but the old man got up no less than three times to use the thunder mug, dribbling into the tin pot while cursing his marshy prostate. Soon after the old man had used the pot for the third time and had resumed his snores in near perfect unison with his wife, Longarm cursed, sat up, and checked his old Ingersoll, tipping the face to the starlit window beside him.

Four-thirty.

He snapped the watch lid closed and rose, still half asleep but nervy as a tortured prisoner from having his cage rattled for the past five hours. Under the circumstances, four-thirty was a perfectly reasonable time for fogging the trail of that skittish showgirl. Hell, he might even be able to catch up to her while she and her pals were still sawing logs in their blanket rolls. . . .

Longarm dressed as quietly as he thought he needed to with his two roommates sounding like a pair of rusty saws over yonder. But as he hefted his rifle and war bag and made for the stairs, feeling his way in the darkness, one of the snores died in a throat while the other continued as before.

The bed creaked to his right.

"Who's there?" croaked the old woman.

Longarm stopped and half-turned. "Just me, ma'am—Deputy Long."

"Be quiet, fer heaven sakes!" she scolded thickly. "I'm a light sleeper!"

"Beg your pardon, ma'am," Longarm grumbled as he resumed cat-footing toward the stairs, tapping the rifle barrel along the floor in front of him so he didn't fall down the stairwell and break his neck.

He made his way down to the first story, stumbling and almost falling only once, then resisted the urge to slam the door to the staircase behind him as he stepped into the near-dark kitchen. Upstairs, Mr. and Mrs. Bergie were raising the rafters like sated sailors once more.

Longarm set three dollars on the table under a sugar bowl, then let himself out into the slightly chill, purple darkness of early morning, his footsteps sounding inordinately loud in the sepulchral silence.

A lone coyote yammered in the distant hills, and the stars sparkled like new-fallen snow.

Resting his rifle barrel on his right shoulder and hefting the war bag his left, Longarm headed toward the heart of the village, trying to remember where he'd spied a livery barn earlier.

Gradually, the Bergies' snores grew silent behind him.

Chapter 10

The livery barn behind Aunt Gert's whorehouse was as dark and quiet as a Methodist church at that early hour. The Mexican answered Longarm's knock on the barn's double doors in his long underwear and boots, wielding an old cap-and-ball pistol. After assuring the man he wasn't there to rob him, Longarm rented a stocky paint gelding that the Mexican swore was a nimble stayer in spite of its ewe-neck and short legs.

At the barn office's rolltop desk, and by a guttering bull's-eye lantern, Longarm scribbled out a note for Billy Vail, in three short sentences updating the chief marshal on his progress at locating the showgirl. The hostler assured Longarm he'd cable the note as soon as the Western Union office opened, thanked him for the gratuity on top of the payment for the horse and the cable, and gave him directions to Owl Creek.

As the hostler slouched back to his cot in the tack room, Longarm heeled the paint into a gallop northeast toward buttes rising like the massive, pale breasts of fat women. An opalescent wash shown along the horizon between rimrocks to his right.

The light grew, erasing the stars, as horse and rider followed an old Army paymaster's route across the undulating desert prairie, passing several long-since-burned-out ranches and a roadhouse Chief Red Cloud must have laid the torch to along with half the military forts in eastern Wyoming and western Dakota, a decade or so ago.

The recent tracks of three wagons showed plainly along the trail, the wheel ruts deeply scored. The constable was right—the showgirls were headed toward Deadwood.

Longarm was three hours northeast of Owl Creek, where the acting troupe had left plenty of sign in the form of warm fire ashes, vegetable tins, and coffee grounds, and reasonably sure he was within an hour of overtaking the wagons, when something flashed in the corner of his left eye. He checked the paint down and, as the horse fidgeted at scolding prairie dogs, turned to look behind him.

The flash shone once more from the crest of a distant rimrock shouldering darkly against the southwestern horizon. A single, bright flash, like that off a spyglass lens.

Longarm sat staring for a good two minutes, shifting his eyes across the rolling sweep of sage-tufted camelbacks behind him, the dry breeze peppering his nose and stinging his eyes.

Whatever had made the sun flash was gone, leaving only the rimrock standing there against the broad, light-blue sky, starkly silent.

Longarm shifted uneasily. Turning forward, he loosened his Winchester in the oiled saddle boot, then heeled the horse forward once more, casting several more glances behind him until he'd made his way over the crest of the next rise.

A half hour later, the paint nickered halfway up a gradual bench. Longarm glanced at the horse, which turned its ugly head and lifted its snout to test the breeze, and nickered again.

It heard or smelled something.

"Gidup!"

Longarm booted the paint to the top of the rise, and drew back on the reins.

A gorge opened before him, steep-walled on both sides,

the other ridge lying about a hundred yards straight north. At the bottom of the gorge, a wide, flat stream glimmered and murmured over rocks between stands of large cottonwoods.

Longarm removed his hat and mopped his brow as he shuttled his gaze left, then right, and froze.

About seventy yards upstream was a rocky ford. Two covered wagons sat on the other side of the stream while one sat motionless in the river, its right rear corner sitting down, as though one wheel were stuck. All of the wagons had large monikers painted on their canvases, but Longarm was too far away to read them from here. Not too far away, however, to see two women lounging around on the far shore and a couple of heads bobbing around on the other side of the wagon.

He glanced behind. No more sun flashes. Except for the occasional prairie dog or dust devil, no movement whatever.

Longarm continued following the wagon trail down a crease in the ridge. At the bottom of the crease, the trail turned into the river. Fifty yards away, the stalled wagon sat where it had been sitting before. Two women in thin chemises and cotton pantaloons were hunkered thigh-deep in the water right of the ford, trying to wedge a long pine pole under the stuck wheel.

Two other girls—a blonde and a chubby redhead—lounged in the shade of the cottonwoods on the far shore, the blonde reading as she reclined against a tree bole, the redhead appearing to nap beneath a pink parasol billowing softly in the breeze.

Longarm figured he could pick Miss Rogers out of the little group easily enough. A miner's wet dream, Friendly had called her, in spite of her decidely smug, self-important disposition. A nicely curved honey-blonde, not a day over twenty-one, with gray-blue eyes, heart-shaped face, and a couple of moles on her neck under her right ear.

Longarm could identify her, all right, but getting her away from her cozy, doubtless protective group of fellow actresses without an embarrassing, possibly life-threatening little dustup—Constable Bergie had mentioned the group's leader freely wielding a double-barreled shotgun—would require some imagination.

None of the girls seemed to have spotted Longarm yet, so he kicked the paint into the stream, holding the mount to a walk and fashioning his best disarming grin. Since the two girls on the shore were preoccupied with reading or sleeping and the two in the water were otherwise occupied with trying to lever the wagon out of its hole, none spotted him till he stopped the paint ten yards off the back of the stalled wagon and raised his voice above the stream's chuckle.

"Need any help, ladies?"

The two in the water jerked their heads to him sharply, eyes flashing fear. The tall one with her brown hair in a bun appeared in her late twenties, early thirties. She looked vaguely familiar, but Longarm couldn't place her. She lunged at the wagon, reaching into the driver's box to produce that short, double-barreled barn-blaster old Bergie had correctly described.

She raised the heavy gun awkwardly in her slender arms, but she somehow raised it quickly, holding it under her left arm while thumbing back the rabbit-eared hammers with the thumb and index fingers of her right hand, and narrowed her bright, blue eyes wickedly. The beauty mark left of her fetching, familiar mouth turned dark.

Longarm winced as the shotgun swung to and fro. He wasn't afraid for himself, as a gun like that was about as deadly as a pickle-loaded slingshot outside of ten feet, but he was concerned that the dark-haired woman was going to cut the girl—a pudgy Mexican whose pear-shaped breasts shone clearly behind her soaked butternut chemise adorned with a small, embroidered rooster—in half.

Longarm raised his hands, palms out and chest high. "Easy with that hog-stopper, miss. I mean you no harm. I was just headin' for Deadwood to spend a couple of days bucking the tiger and spinning the roulette wheel, when I spied you down here under what appeared to be some duress. Can I give you a hand and get you back on your way?"

The tall woman stood slightly behind and left of the pretty little Mexican, who didn't seem to care that her breasts were nearly as exposed as her nose. She seemed relieved at the offer of assistance. Meanwhile, aiming the shotgun with both hands, the dark-haired gal regarded Longarm from between slitted eyelids.

"You trailin' us?"

Just then, Longarm's gut burned as he recognized the gal as an icy female outlaw he'd once tussled with in California. She'd gotten away, and under different circumstances, he'd be tempted to haul the wildcat in. But the dwarf's chippie was his primary concern now.

He tried not to complicate matters by betraying his recognition.

"I reckon since we're on the same trail and you were *ahead* of me, I was *behind* you. But, no, I wasn't intentionally *followin'* you." Longarm flicked his gaze across the stream, where the other two girls now stood along the bank, staring toward him. He smiled and waved at the two on shore, but he might as well have been waving at stones.

The brunette glanced at the Mexican, who shifted her brown eyes between her and Longarm hopefully. The brunette lowered the shotgun slightly to glance at the other two behind her, then turned back to Longarm.

"Amber was reading instead of driving the wagon, and she let the wheel here slip off the ford and into a hole." The brunette ran her gaze up and down Longarm speculatively, shifted her weight from foot to foot in the water, then dropped the shotgun's barrel and gestured to the pine pole, one end of which was wedged beneath the wagon's right rear wheel while the other stuck about four feet above the stream. "We'd be obliged . . ."

"Anything I can do to help." Longarm dismounted, and looped the paint's reins through a canvas cover hitch on the wagon box. When he'd removed his hat, frock, and gunbelt, tossing all three over the wagon's tailgate, he waded over to where the brunette and the Mexican stood in the stream rippling around their pantaloons.

"You don't mind if I hang onto my gut-shredder, do you?" the brunette asked, her eyes flashing ironically. "Since we don't know you and all . . ."

Longarm studied her for a moment. Having recognized him, was she toying with him? When she merely backed up, eyes cool as she held the shotgun's barrel down, he nodded politely at her and the Mexican girl, then glanced at the other two standing along the stream, looking toward him with careful interest.

He squatted down and inspected the wheel. It was wedged between two boulders, the water rising to the hub. The girls had the pole placed correctly, so he stepped back, wrapped his hands around the pole, leaned down hard, and promptly cracked it.

"Madre Maria!" exclaimed the Mexican, squeezing her face in her hands and shaking her head, causing her breasts to wag like dog tails, and the embroidered rooster to leap and bound.

"Ah, shit!" exclaimed the brunette huskily, placing her free hand on her hip with disgust.

Longarm's momentum had soaked his entire right arm in the river, but he gained his feet, grinning. "The pole wasn't a bad choice . . . if it hadn't been so long. I got another idea. Why don't you two hop up in the driver's box, and pull the mules back toward the shallow part of the river when I give a yell?"

"Don't you want one of us to help?" asked the brunette dourly.

Longarm took advantage of the opportunity to run his eyes across each woman's soaked chemise once more. The brunette casually crossed her arms over her breasts and smirked. There was no recognition on her face. After all, he hadn't seen her in five years.

"I can handle it," Longarm said.

When the women had climbed into the driver's box, he snugged his left shoulder under the wagon box near the tailgate. He set his boots in the rocky streambed and, when he was sure his boots wouldn't slip, ordered the women to hoorah the mules.

As the mules leaned into their collars, braying, and the wagon lurched forward, Longarm heaved straight up with his left shoulder, both hands clutching the undercarriage. He stretched his lips back from his teeth as he flexed his legs.

He was surprised to find that the wagon wasn't as heavy as he'd figured, considering that women weren't generally known for traveling light, and that it wasn't too badly stuck either. In fact, he didn't think he'd caused any vertebrae to bulge from his spine before the wheel rose up out of the hole with a creak and a thump, water sluicing off the spokes.

The wagon clattered ahead onto the ford.

The pretty Mexican gal clapped and peered behind as she exclaimed, *"Oh, el hombre alto nos ha ahorrado!"*

She was happy as hell the tall gent had saved their bacon.

Longarm stepped onto the ford, the river splashing around his stovepipe boots, and waved them forward, the paint following but jerking its head at the splashing water. "Keep on goin', and I'll catch up to you on the other side."

He trudged out of the stream a minute behind the wagon, then sat on a rock to remove each boot and pour out the water. He contemplated his next move, now that he was in the females' good graces, then reached into his shirt pocket for a three-for-a-nickel cheroot. Happy to find all five of his remaining cigars still dry, he bit the end off one, lit it with a dry lucifer, then pushed up from the rock.

Boots still soaked and squeaking with each step, he strode up to the right side of the wagon, where the Mexican girl and the other two who'd remained on shore stood in a close group near the driver's box. They were conversing in hushed tones amongst themselves and with the brunette still perched in the driver's box.

Probably discussing whether to pay this drifting gambler for his services or bid him adieu with only a smile and a wave.

It wasn't hard to pick out his quarry. Tall, slender, and

fresh-faced, Miss Amber Rogers stood on the far side of the group in a plain shirtwaist and light-green traveling skirt. Her honey-blond hair was pulled up in a loose bun atop her head, with several haylike wisps brushing her cheeks and neck. Her heart-shaped face with distinguishing moles was tan from traveling under the prairie sun.

Suddenly, the pretty Mexican gal ran toward him, clapping her hands and grinning brightly, still seemingly unaware of how much of her showed under her soaked underwear clinging to her like a see-through second skin.

"El Brazo Largo," she exclaimed. "You have saved us!"

"Oh, I wouldn't go that far, miss." He'd just removed his cigar from his mouth, but quickly replaced it when the lithe Mexican girl bounded off her feet, wrapping her arms around his neck, her long legs around his waist. He snaked his arms under her thighs so she wouldn't fall and, grunting with the effort of holding her, said around the cigar in his teeth, "I'm sure you would have gotten the wagon out of that hole sooner or later. I'm just glad I came along to help."

A shadow moved in the grass to his right. He swung around suddenly, evoking a startled yelp from the Mexican girl in his arms. He thrust her straight forward, evoking another yowl from both her and the older brunette, who'd been stealing up behind him, swinging her double-barreled barnblaster like a club at his head.

As the shotgun smacked his right arm, he heaved the Mexican girl out away from him, and into the spread arms of the blue-eyed brunette. The shotgun thumped into the grass at Longarm's feet.

Both women fell in a heap, the Mexican atop the brunette, who was cursing and yelling, "Longarm, you son of a fucking bitch!"

Chapter 11

Longarm stepped back from the women flailing around in the brush between him and the stream, and spread his feet, rubbing his upper arm where the shotgun had smacked it. "Hello, Judith. How the hell you been? I was kinda hopin' you wouldn't recognize me."

"How could I *not* remember that famous mug of yours, Longarm?"

He'd known Judith Taylor back in San Francisco, when she'd been dancing at the Barbary Special when she wasn't cavorting with the counterfeiters he'd been sent to lasso. He hadn't gotten a chance to send her to the federal pen, however, since her considerably less slippery partners had preoccupied him until she, a minor player in the scheme, had lit a shuck for parts unknown.

That was five years ago. Since her part in the operation had been much smaller than that of her male counterparts, she hadn't been worth going after. Besides, he'd figured she was in a ravine or unmarked grave somewhere, which was where most women with her sharp tongue and lawless cunning ended up.

As she struggled back to her feet, her broad, clean-lined face flushed with fury, Longarm removed the double-barreled derringer from his vest pocket and aimed it at her chest to discourage her from any more roughhousing.

Her eyes dropped to the gun, and she stopped, crossed her arms over her pert bosom, which, like the Mexican girl's, clearly showed beneath her soaked chemise. "That third time you ogled my breasts and acquired your trademark shit-eating grin, I knew it was you."

"What a coincidence. I recognized you the second time you gave me the twice-over looking for a fat wallet or a money belt."

Judith Taylor glanced at the honey-blonde standing with the pudgy redhead near the wagon, looking toward Longarm anxiously. "She doesn't want to testify."

"It doesn't matter if she *wants* to testify or not. I've got a subpoena that says she *has* to." Longarm bunched his face as he stared at Judith skeptically. "Besides, what's it to you if she testifies or not? I doubt even an old albeit pretty sinner like you would throw in with *that* smelly little reprobate!"

He couldn't wrap his mind around the blonde succumbing to the dwarf's wiles either.

"I walk the straight and narrow now, Longarm," Judith said, glancing at one of the wagons, large pink letters painted on the canvas announcing JUDITH JASMINE'S TRAVELING ACTRESSES. "I make an honest living, and these girls are part of it. I take care of them and they take care of me."

"That's real sweet. What's the *real* reason?"

Judith furled her brows and opened her mouth, then closed it again. Flushing, she glanced at Amber Rogers clutching her yellow-covered book like she was trying to rip it in half.

Turning back to Longarm, she lowered her voice. "She's a big draw for the men. She reads romantic poetry and sings sad songs on stage." The troupe leader raised her eyebrows. "She's become quite a draw. The men can't get enough. In fact, a saloon owner in Deadwood has contracted my entire show for the rest of the summer. He's paid half in advance. If I don't show with Amber in tow, he'll almost certainly cancel the contract."

"Look," Longarm said, growing weary with the whole encounter and yearning to head back the way he'd come, with his witness on a short leash. "If you give me any more trouble, Judith, I'm liable to bring you in too."

She lifted her chin smugly. "No jury would convict me after five years. Not a face like mine." She lifted her chin and batted her lashes. "Besides, all the *real* paperhangers are in the pen. I was just their laundress."

Longarm wanted no part in running Judith out to San Francisco for a trial he'd probably lose for lack of evidence and witnesses after five years, but bluffing was an effective tool in law enforcement as well as in five-card stud. He narrowed his eyes as he said evenly, "Wanna powwow with my boss about it?"

The wide-mouthed, high-busted brunette scowled at him as the Mexican girl sat on the ground beside her, sulkily inspecting her left elbow, which she'd scratched when Longarm had dumped her in the coarse grass along the stream.

Judith dropped her chin as well as her arms, inviting another gander at her chest. She nibbled her upper lip as she sauntered toward him, throwing her hips from side to side and thrusting her pink-tipped breasts out. "Custis, we shared a special time together. Remember? When you were using me to try to corral Logan and the others?"

She stopped about a foot away from the uncocked derringer he now aimed at her belly and gave him a direct, smoky look. "A *very* special time. I think of it often." Her lips twisted slightly, seductively. "If I remember correctly, *you* enjoyed it *immensely*. So immensely, in fact, that I bet you'd consider reliving it . . . if we came to some sort of agreement. . . ."

Longarm laughed. "You mean, for a quick romp in the weeds with you minus your underwear, I let the girl go?"

Judith's voice sharpened slightly, as did her smile. "I see your wits haven't dulled one iota in the past five years, Deputy Long." She cleared her throat and added with a tolerant air, "To put it more delicately, for a rapturously romantic night with me by a quiet fire along the river, you tell the sheriff back in Chugwater that you simply couldn't find Miss Rogers. She just plumb disappeared!"

Longarm stared at her skeptically. He glanced at Amber Rogers, who was regarding him beseechingly, her cheeks ashen, then returned his gaze to Judith. "Have her pack a bag and crawl on the back of my horse. We're outta here. I'll do you the favor, for no fuck or even a blow job, of seeing that, after she testifies in Chugwater, she's returned to your high-class traveling troupe pronto."

The woman pursed her lips and tightened her jaws, rolling her eyes around. "Ladies, it appears that this thick son of a bitch won't listen to reason. Amber, hop up on the wagon and hightail it outta here while we *distract* him!" Glancing at the pudgy redhead, she said, "Camille, you stay here."

Longarm made a pained expression and dropped his arms to his side. "Judith, goddamnit, the girl's comin' with me, and there ain't no if's, ands, or butts—*uhffff!*"

The air had burst from his lungs as the woman stepped forward in a blur of motion and, gritting her teeth savagely, buried her right knee in his groin.

Longarm groaned as he dropped to his knees in the grass while clutching his crotch with both hands and cursing himself for letting his guard down. He felt his face turn as hot as Sonoran desert rocks at midday.

He'd been kneed in the oysters before, but Judith was apparently an old pro at fighting dirty. She couldn't have hit him any more directly had he painted a bull's-eye over his fly. His balls felt as though they'd already swollen up to the size of baseballs while throbbing and flinging sharp, poison-tipped javelins of pain from his loins to deep within his belly.

For a second, he thought he was going to throw up. Then he felt Judith's hands pulling his hair, tugging his head up while she swung her right leg back, intending to smash that dangerous knee into his face. He sobered instantly and, snarling furiously, bolted forward, driving his head into Judith's own crotch.

She gave a surprised grunt and a clipped scream as he rose off his heels, lifting her two feet off the ground and bulling her straight back to the edge of the stream and laying her out in a damp, dusty pile of buffeting pantaloons, chemise, and hair.

"Oh!" she exclaimed, bunching her lips with fury as she pushed up on her elbows. *"Fucker!"*

His balls throbbing hotly, Longarm looked down to see that he'd somehow held onto his derringer. As he raised it, intending to drill a slug into the ground beside Judith, to take some starch out of her panties, the Mexican girl leaped onto his back, screaming Spanish epithets and pummeling his head with her tiny brown fists.

Longarm turned to the stream, and, bending forward, twisting his torso, and throwing up his right arm, he flung the raging polecat into the water. Above the girl's thrashing and splashing rose the wooden clatter of a wagon. Longarm turned to see the covered Conestoga he'd freed from the stream bouncing along the trail climbing toward a crease in the rising eastern buttes.

Between him and the wagon, twenty feet away, the fat redhead, wearing a frilly green, low-cut dress and canvas shoes, stood holding her closed, pink parasol in both hands before her, puffing her cheeks out and staring at Longarm with anxious challenge in her eyes.

He'd begun moving toward her when Judith sprang off her heels, swinging a rock in her right hand, her loose hair bouncing around her face and jostling breasts. She stopped as he wheeled toward her, and crouched before him, shifting her weight from foot to foot while hefting the stone and smiling crookedly.

"I'll kill you before I'll let you take that girl!"

There was nothing like a kick in the balls to rile a man, and Longarm felt like a grizzly bear with a singed ass. He was in no mood to pull any punches. Lunging toward Judith, he grabbed the rock as she swung it toward his head.

"No!" she bellowed.

Longarm twisted her wrist sharply down. Her fingers opened, and the rock fell to the ground with a thump.

At the same time, the Mexican girl leaped on Longarm again and went to work with her fists, grunting and sighing as though she were nearing climax.

"Kill him!" Judith screamed.

Wheeling on one foot while shoving the brunette aside with one forearm, he tried to dislodge the Mexican girl with the other. In the periphery of his vision, he saw the fat redhead run toward him, extending her parasol like a saber and bunching her lips with fury.

"I'll get him, Miss Judith!" The redhead had a body like a corn-fed heifer and a voice like a mule, and her jowls shook like fresh suet. "I'll trim his wick but good!"

Longarm was glad that Billy Vail couldn't bear witness to this humiliating predicament—the chief marshal's senior deputy trying to fight off three gals without actually *killing* them, but not wanting himself to be turned down with the snakes either.

Longarm spun the Mex into the redhead, throwing the redhead into the river. With a savage grunt, he shook the Mexican off as well.

"Bastardo!" the girl screamed as she flew ass over teakettle into the drink, landing in a gently swirling pool between boulders with a hollow splash.

Longarm turned from the river. Judith Taylor stalked toward him and raised her right arm straight out from her shoulder. She was holding Longarm's derringer in her hand. Grinning savagely as she moved within ten feet, she yelled, "You're out of my hair once and for all, you son of a bitch!"

The peashooter popped and smoked.

Longarm ducked, hearing the small-caliber slug curl the air as it patted down a rooster tail at the top of his head before slamming into a rock in the river behind him.

"Die!" Judith screamed through clenched teeth.

But before she could cock the peashooter again, Longarm bolted forward. He grabbed the hand holding the derringer and gave the woman a dancelike spin into the river while wrenching the pistol free.

Her yowl as she slammed into the fat redhead was clipped by the splash.

As Judith came up sputtering and blowing water from between her lips, Longarm looked at the other two lolling about the shallows to her left. The fat redhead was on her knees, her lips bleeding as she wiped water from her eyes and bawled.

The Mexican girl sat a few feet away but closer to shore, legs spread most unladylike, leaning on her arms, the fight out of her. The girl's torn chemise lay about her waist, fully revealing her pointy, brown breasts glistening wet in the sunlight. She scowled up at Longarm, her lips set in a pout.

Longarm looked at Judith, who faced him now on her hands and knees, drawing air into her lungs and eyeing him like a hungry but half-resigned she-wolf.

Longarm drew a breath and set his jaws. "Stay there."

"And if we don't?"

Longarm raised the derringer. Judith screamed, ducked, and covered her face with both hands as the peashooter popped. The slug ricochetted off a rock to her left with a loud, angry bark.

Slowly, she raised her head and peeked at him from between her fingers, her eyes bright with fear.

Longarm turned and peered east. The wagon was crowning the pass between two chalky, eroded buttes, its dusty canvas billowing in the warm breeze. The dry wheel hubs barked and the wooden bed creaked and groaned as the load shifted. The rented paint horse followed doggedly, dust lifting around its hocks.

Longarm said, "Shit."

He winced as he headed off for the crease, jogging, his bruised balls jostling painfully inside his underwear. Ahead, the wagon and the paint disappeared down the other side of the pass.

Longarm cursed again and quickened his pace, drawing his tweed pants away from his crotch. A simple assignment, Billy Vail had called it.

A simple assignment, Longarm's ass.

Breaking a sweat in the hot sun, his shirt and vest pasting against his chest and back, his feet swelling inside the low-heeled cavalry boots, he slogged up the pass and stopped. He sleeved sweat and mud from his forehead and peered down the other side.

He sighed, relieved to see the wagon heading toward another, higher pass beyond the one he was on. The mules were still moving at a good clip down the grade below Longarm, but they'd slow considerably when they started up the next, steeper hill.

He spat dust and sweat from his lips, then started down the other side of the pass, catching up to his horse and the wagon's tailgate five minutes later. The wheels churned the floury dust as the wagon slowed to a crawl, the mules chuffing and braying as they slogged up the steep incline, the box groaning as the wheels bounced over ruts and chuckholes.

"Go, damn you!" a girl's tormented voice rose from the driver's box. "Go, damnit . . . *hur-ree!*"

Walking casually along beside his horse, Longarm grabbed his coat and hat off the tailgate. He donned the hat and threw his coat over his saddle horn. When he'd strapped his gunbelt around his waist, he walked up along the wagon's left side to the driver's box. The blonde stood in the box, whipping the reins against the mules' backs. As Longarm drew even with her, she turned toward him sharply, eyes snapping wide.

"No!" she screamed as Longarm reached up with both hands. He set the brake, then grabbed her harshly and pulled her across the wheel and over his right shoulder.

She kicked and screamed and pummeled his back with her fists as he hauled her like a sack of cracked corn toward the wagon's rear. "Put me down, you bastard! He's gonna kill me, you fool!"

"Miss Amber Rogers or whatever your *real* name is," Longarm said, dropping to one knee as he laid her out on the ground beside his horse, "I am hereby officially serving you a subpoena to testify at the court trial of one . . . uh . . . the dwarf. I'm sure his given name's on the subpoena, but I reckon you already know it, bein' the little bastard's darling and all." He bruquely turned her belly-down, then planted one boot on her back as he reached up and grabbed the lariat from his saddle.

She sobbed and begged him to let her go, warned him that if he took her back toward Chugwater she'd be dead in hours . . . that *they'd* be dead in hours. Longarm only half listened. He was hot, his feet ached, and his balls throbbed. He was done trifling with females.

In under three minutes, he'd hogtied her with the lariat and laid her belly-down across the paint's back, uncomfortably wedged between the saddle horn and the horse's neck.

"Let me go!" she cried as Longarm swung into the leather and neck-reined the horse back toward the stream. "Oh, please let me go. The saddle horn is pinching my lungs . . . and he'll kill me for sure!"

She begged and pleaded and cried all the way to the stream, her voice shaking with the horse's lumbering gait. Longarm paid her no attention other than to note that he couldn't let her ride that way very long, for she'd surely be dead by sundown.

He snorted devilishly.

An easy assignment, bullshit!

As Longarm approached the stream, he saw Judith, the still-bare-breasted Mex, and the fat redhead sprawled in the grass near where Longarm had thrown them in. They looked like schoolgirls who'd been kicked out of school for the afternoon. The fat redhead dabbed at her lips with the hem of her green dress.

Regarding him owlishly as he put the paint into the stream, Judith lifted her hand in a lewd gesture.

The paint splashed across the ford, Miss Amber Rogers grunting and bawling, her blond hair flopping across Longarm's right stirrup. He tipped his hat to the three women on the shore.

"*Hasta luego,* ladies!"

Chapter 12

The dwarf was snoring loudly and with infuriating abandon
as Jim Friendly poured himself a cup of coffee at his small,
sheet-iron cookstove, then sauntered back to his cluttered
desk and sank down in his swivel chair.

He glanced over his shoulder, into the cell where the dwarf
slept with his hat over his eyes, his hawk nose protruding beneath the brim. The dwarf's lumpy chest rose as he sucked a
deep, languorous breath. His chapped lips pooched out
slightly as he blew out the breath on a long, resonating snore.

Friendly snorted angrily and turned toward his desk,
glowering into his coffee cup as he reached for his bourbon
bottle.

"Little fucker."

He plucked the wooden cork from the bottle, and tipped a
finger of the bourbon into the coffee. "I wonder how deep
he'd nap if I went over there and raked my pistol across his
cage every five minutes." The only reason he didn't was the
little demon was even louder awake, making demands and
spewing his verbal poison.

Friendly stirred the coffee with a pencil, then corked the
bottle and lifted the cup to his lips, blowing on it. "Fry his
nerves like mine are fried . . ."

Friendly sipped the spiked coffee and, trying to ignore

the dwarf's snores, wondered where Longarm was and if the federal deputy had picked up the girl yet. If she was still alive, that is . . .

If she wasn't, or if Longarm couldn't get her back for the trial, Friendly's goose was cooked. The dwarf would keep his stranglehold on Chugwater, and the town itself would soon be nothing more than an outlaw hollow, governed by the gun. And the sheriff, unable to hold off the onslaught of outlaws as well as the dwarf's own hired killers, would be dead.

His daughter, Mary Lou, would no doubt be killed, or worse. . . .

Friendly snapped the pencil he still held in his hands—the crack echoing like the report of a small-caliber pistol.

The dwarf fell silent in mid-snore, gurgled, grunted, then resumed snoring. The Chugwater sheriff tossed the two halves of the pencil against the far wall with a curse.

Someone tapped on the jailhouse's heavy, timbered door.

Friendly reached for the Colt Navy on his right hip, curled his fingers around the worn walnut butt, but left the pistol in its holster. He stared at the door, turned his head slightly, and squinted one eye. "Who is it?"

"St. Paul," said a British-accented voice on the other side of the door.

Friendly cursed and heaved himself out of his chair. He took a sip of the coffee and bourbon, then walked over to the window, sliding the feed-sack curtain aside with his right hand while angling a glance toward the stoop fronting the door.

He chuckled wryly as he released the curtain, then stomped over to the door, tripped the lever latch, and drew it open. Friendly stood scrutinizing the pair before him—a skinny, dapper albino and a heavy-breasted brunette in a spangled dress and picture hat from which a plumb-colored ostrich feather jutted.

The albino held a fawn-colored umbrella over himself and the girl. She smiled shyly up at Friendly, and shrugged, the low-cut frock revealing a good half of her creamy bosom. The albino grinned, his small, straight teeth showing yellow between his spread pink lips.

Friendly snorted. What was he running here—a goddamn freak show? "Where's the one-armed juggler?" Without waiting for a response, he wheeled and, walking back toward his desk, cleared his throat loudly. "Wake up, sleeping beauty. Your *attorney's* here!"

Friendly grabbed the key ring off his court docket and sauntered over to the dwarf's cell. The dwarf stopped snoring, grabbed his hat off his chest, and jerked his head up, looking around groggily, smacking his lips, and blinking.

The albino and the girl—J. Mortimer St. Paul and the little Russian whore whose name Friendly couldn't remember, but whom the dwarf had imported from Laramie because she sang spellbinding songs in her native tongue and was a master at fellatio—crossed the room to the cell block. The albino stopped near Friendly and closed the umbrella, holding it low in his kid-gloved right hand.

The rabbit eyes regarded the sheriff with mockery as the man said in his heavy British accent, "Aren't you going to frisk us, Sheriff?"

Friendly shook his head. "I hope you're heeled, so I can blow both your and *his* brains all over that cell block wall back yonder." He shifted his eyes to the whore, who stared at him blankly, uncomprehending. "Beg your pardon, miss."

"Just open the fuckin' door, Friendly," the dwarf ordered, curling his beringed sausage fingers around the bars.

Friendly turned toward the little man, his jaws and eyes hardening, an angry flush rising beneath his leathery tan.

"Now, now, Sheriff," said J. Mortimer St. Paul, whom the dwarf had brought in from Omaha when Friendly had started regularly hauling the little man before the circuit judge about a year ago. "You know as well as I do that Mr. Turley has the privilege of a once-a-day visit from his attorney."

Titus Turley was the dwarf's given name.

Keeping his hard gaze locked on the dwarf, the sheriff moved to the door, shoved the key in the lock, and turned it. He stepped back, and the lawyer and the girl stepped inside. Friendly had started to object to the girl's presence, but he saw no point in arguing. Let the little bastard stare at her tits all he wanted; the frustration would serve him right.

The three stood staring at Friendly expectantly until he closed the door. As the lawyer and his client began whispering, Friendly sauntered back to his desk, threw the keys onto the docket, sank back in his chair, and raised the coffee and bourbon to his lips.

He'd taken another sip when he heard a belt buckle clink and clothes rustle. He turned to see the dwarf standing beside his cot, broadcloth trousers bunched around his hairy, knobby knees, shirttails hanging to his thighs.

The whore knelt on the floor before him, her head only a little lower than his. She could have been waiting to be granted absolution from a priest.

Friendly said, "Hey, what the hell do you think you're doing?"

The dwarf jerked his head toward the sheriff and said with an air of strained patience, "She's gonna blow me while I talk with my lawyer."

"Like hell!" Friendly lurched to his feet, grabbed the key, and stalked over to the cell.

"I know my rights, you son of a bitch! I can have a blow job if I want one." The dwarf turned his head to the albino sitting in the chair across from the cot, legs crossed, his derby on his knee. "Tell him my rights!"

The albino opened his mouth to speak, but Friendly cut him off. "Not in my jailhouse!" He opened the door, reached in, and pulled the girl to her feet. To the dwarf, Friendly said, "Why don't I bring in a canopied bed and a three-piece band? A bottle of French wine perhaps?"

"You buyin'?"

The whore gave a startled cry as Friendly pulled her out of the cell and nearly out of her shoes. "What the hell do you think I'm running here—a whorehouse?"

"You don't have that kind of class or business sense, Friendly!" the dwarf shouted.

The sheriff threw the whore out of the jailhouse, then turned back to the dwarf glaring at him through the bars of his cell, his blue eyes large and bright, his face flushed with fury.

"I'm gonna enjoy killin' you, Friendly," he said, throwing his head back and speaking with hushed menace. "I'm gonna enjoy watchin' you die *slow*!"

Friendly sat down in his chair and squinted one eye at the dwarf. "I'm gonna enjoy you tryin'."

When the sheriff had turned toward his desk and opened his court docket, he heard the dwarf pull his pants up and buckle his belt. There was a squawk as the little man sat down on his cot.

"So, Mort," the dwarf said, loudly enough for Friendly to hear. "That tall drink of water of a deputy United States marshal dead yet?"

Friendly turned toward the cell. The albino was looking at Friendly, his pasty cheeks flushed slightly, his face tense, his half-open mouth issuing no words.

The dwarf followed the lawyer's gaze to the sheriff, and chuckled hoarsely. "What're you worried about, Mort? You're my lawyer, and it's against the law for him to eavesdrop." The dwarf turned back to the albino. "So, spit it out. That federal eat a pill he couldn't digest?"

The albino shuttled his gaze back and forth between the dwarf and Friendly. He cleared his throat and said barely loudly enough for Friendly to hear, "Uh . . . no. That didn't work out."

"Shit!" The dwarf lifted his chin and scratched his neck, stretching his lips back from his teeth. "Have we located my *friend* yet, or do we need to up the . . . uh"—the dwarf glanced at Friendly, still glaring at them from his desk—"finder's fee?"

The albino shifted uncomfortably in his seat, still shuttling his glance between his employer and the local lawman. Finally, fiddling with his hat, he said, "No, we don't have word on her, uh, fate yet either. On my counsel and per our last conversation, Mr. Paxton has sent . . . emissaries . . . toward Coyote Flats."

"Emissaries, huh?" The dwarf chuckled. "Good. I like emissaries. I like emissaries real good." He glanced at

Friendly again, grinned, then leaned forward and made a show of casually scratching his back as he said, "Just in case those emissaries aren't as effective as we hope, startin' tomorrow have Paxton send men into the buttes around town. Make a big circle!"

The dwarf turned toward Friendly and grinned so wide that nearly all his overlarge teeth shone in his craggy, repugnant face. "We wouldn't want any unsavory characters ridin' into Chugwater and givin' the local law any trouble now, would we, Mort? You oughta be grateful you got a man like me around, Sheriff. A man who takes pride in his town and has enough men to help you local badge-toters enforce the laws. Yessir!"

Friendly's stomach burned, but he forced a smile. "At the next town council meeting, I'm gonna suggest we give you a special citation, Dwarf. We'll give you a plaque to set over your grave—a plaque sayin', 'Here lies the meanest, smallest, ugliest piece of worm-infested shit that ever choked a dog off a gut wagon. May he burn in hell!'"

Later, when the lawyer had left, leaving the dwarf with a thick Havana cigar, which he smoked sitting on the side of his cot, elbows on his knees, child-sized cowboy boots dangling six inches above the floor, the dwarf said, "How old's your daughter, Jim? You mind if I call you Jim? We been together so long now, I feel we've become . . . close. . . ."

Friendly was standing by the window facing the street left of the timbered door, leaning with one shoulder on the brick wall, holding a fresh cup of coffee and bourbon in his right hand. He'd been watching the slow afternoon wagon and horse traffic kick up dust in the waning sunlight, wondering about Longarm and the girl.

He didn't turn to the dwarf. His voice was a grizzlylike growl. "A word of advice, dwarf? Turn your thoughts away from my daughter."

"I was just thinkin'," the dwarf said behind him. "She's gonna be mighty lonely out on the farm by herself . . . once all this . . . you know . . . plays out. She might consider movin' into town, come to work for me at the Dwarf House."

The dwarf sat at the edge of his cot, casually swinging his

short legs and studying the gray coal at the end of his cigar. His cell was filled with aromatic smoke, which webbed through the bars into Friendly's office.

"I told you to turn your thoughts away from my daughter, dwarf."

The dwarf turned toward him as though he hadn't heard the threat. "Pretty little thing, ain't she? She could make a good livin' over to the Dwarf House."

The dwarf's eyes glittered delightedly as Friendly moved toward him.

The dwarf raised the hand with the cigar in it. "Hell, I ain't tryin' to get your goat, Jim. I'm just tryin' to put your mind at ease. You wouldn't have to worry about her." The dwarf's flat eyes gained an icy light, like those of a doll outside on a sunny day. "I might even take her under my very own personal wing. She'd have a special place in my own, uh . . . quarters. . . ."

As Friendly passed his desk, he grabbed the key ring without looking at it. He glared, nostrils flaring, at the little man still sitting at the edge of the cot—a demon-faced abomination in the body of a wizened child. An image of Mary Lou in a spangled dress and with feathers in her hair—sitting on the dwarf's knee as the little man smoked a cigar like the one he smoked now—flashed through the sheriff's mind. Nausea welled in his gut. A red haze grew before his eyes.

"I warned you."

"Jim," the dwarf said, smiling unctuously, "I've got your daughter's best interests in mind. I mean, with looks like hers, why let her molder out there on your dusty old ranch?"

Staring down at the dwarf grinning up at him, Friendly shoved the key in the lock. His hand was shaking. He turned the lock, opened the door, and leaving the key in the lock, stepped into the cell, eyes blazing, the muscles in his face hard as stones.

The dwarf held his gaze. He poked the thick cigar between his thin, wet lips, and puffed smoke out the side of his mouth. His evil snake eyes crossed behind the smoke veil, slightly bloodshot. His pink lips were cracked and scaly.

Friendly bounded toward him and lunged down to wrap

his right hand around the dwarf's thick neck. The dwarf had anticipated the manuever and, at the last second, dropped the cigar and parried Friendly's jutting hand with both of his. The little man bolted up and, clutching Friendly's right wrist in his surprisingly strong right hand, rammed his head into Friendly's gut.

Friendly grunted and fell, twisting at the waist, against the sour-smelling cot. He saw the dwarf's elbow blurring toward him too late. The elbow smashed against Friendly's jaw, and then the little man, grunting and cursing under his breath, had his hand on Friendly's holstered revolver.

"You're gonna die, Friendly, and I'm gonna bend your daughter over a pork barrel every night and every—" The dwarf had the Remington half out of the holster when Friendly closed his own right hand over the dwarf's and rammed his left fist into the dwarf's chin.

"Unhh!" the dwarf cried as he stumbled back toward the rear of the cell, fell, and piled up against the wall. "Bastard, I think you broke my jaw!"

Friendly stood over him, holding the revolver low in his right hand. He thumbed the hammer back and angled the revolver at the dwarf's bulbous, pockmarked forehead. "That ain't all I'm gonna break." The fatigue and the fury and the worry had cut him thin as doeskin. With one shot, it would all be over.

The dwarf sat with his back to the brick wall and kicked his boots like an enraged child. "You broke my fuckin' jaw, you son of a bitch!"

Friendly squinted one eye and aimed down the barrel. The dwarf glanced up at him, saw the gun, then lifted his arms and spread his hands before his face, pressing one cheek against the wall.

"No! Friendly, goddamnit, I was just joshin'!"

Friendly began taking up the slack in his index finger, squeezing the trigger.

"No!" the dwarf wailed. "You can't kill me, goddamnit. *I got rights!"*

The jailhouse door clicked and a boot thumped on the

puncheons. "Pa, I'm all through. You wanna ride back—?"

Friendly turned a glance out the open cell door. Mary Lou stood holding the outside door open, staring back at her father, frowning. She'd been filling their buckboard at the general store, and she was wearing range clothes and a broad-brimmed felt hat. Her suntanned face was dusty.

Friendly turned back to the dwarf on the floor before him. "Go on outside, Mary Lou. I'll be along in a minute."

"Speak sense to your pa, girl," the dwarf shrieked, still holding his hands in front of his face as he stretched his horrified gaze toward the outer office. "He's gonna kill me!"

"Go on out, Mary Lou."

"Pa, what's goin' on?"

Boots thumped, and the cell door chirped. Out the corner of his left eye, Friendly saw the girl move up behind him.

"Call him off!" the dwarf pleaded, his Missouri accent suddenly more pronounced. "He's gone loco as a peach orchard sow! He's gone kill me!"

Friendly stared down at the dwarf, the fire still burning in his gut. The dwarf stared back at him from behind his raised hands, his pupils expanding and contracting, sweat streaming down his face.

Mary Lou squeezed his arm. "Holster the iron, Pa."

Friendly jerked his head toward her. "I told you to—!"

Mary Lou held her father's gaze, her own eyes unwavering. "It ain't your way, Pa. You gotta wait for the judge."

Friendly turned back to the dwarf and jabbed the gun toward him. The little man's right eye twitched as both hands shook, the fingers curved like claws.

Friendly removed his finger from the Remington's trigger, depressed the hammer, and returned the revolver to its holster. Slowly, the dwarf lowered his hands, though the wary, vaguely befuddled expression remained on his face.

"Soon as Lon and Scratch get back from supper," Friendly told his daughter evenly, "I'll ride home with you in the wagon."

As the sheriff turned and followed his daughter out of the cell, the dwarf heaved a phlegmy sigh behind him.

Chapter 13

Fifteen minutes after leaving the demonic Judith Taylor and the two other showgirls—and tired of hearing Amber Rogers grunt and sob as she lay sprawled uncomfortably across the horse before him—Longarm turned the paint off the trail and followed the sloping prairie into a stand of cottonwoods shading a shallow stream.

Chickadees peeped in the sun-bronzed leaves, and crows took flight, bellowing raucously as they winged toward the sandstone ridge rising on the stream's other side.

The showgirl's whining, complimented by occasional shouted demands and terrified shrieks, had degenerated into a steady string of sobs as Longarm stopped the horse at the edge of the stream and stepped down from the saddle. He dropped the reins, then reached up and eased the girl down over the paint's left stirrup.

She continued sobbing, no longer fighting the lariat he'd used to loosely hogtie her, as he lay her down by the stream. As she slumped sideways onto the wet sand, her hands tied behind her back, her tethered ankles drawn partway up to her bottom, which was showing taut and round under her soiled green traveling skirt, he almost felt sorry for her.

Almost.

His balls still bemoaned the groining Judith had given

him while Miss Rogers had fled in the wagon. His head still ached from the pretty Mex's surprisingly potent fists.

He hunkered down beside Miss Rogers and said above the stream's chuckle and the swish of the breeze in the trees, "If you promise not to run away, I'll untie you. If you can't behave yourself, you'll ride all the way back to Chugwater in the same position."

Her left cheek pressed against the sand, tears streaking her round, dusty face, she bunched her lips and said through clenched teeth, "You have no right to do this to me. I've done nothing *wrong*!"

"You tried to flee a federal subpoena. Uncle Sam, both local and federal, gets right prickly about that sorta behavior. Now, I know you haven't killed anybody, and I also know that no one would know that you know who *did* kill somebody if you hadn't done your civic duty and told Jim Friendly. But now that the cat's outta the bag, and you promised to haul your ass back to Chugwater for the court trial, the fat's in the fire!"

She lifted her head to glare up at him, her light-brown eyes flashing rage and terror. "I thought I could just *write* and tell the sheriff what happened. If I'd known I had to go *back* there, I never would have done anything but hightail it the hell outta the country—which I was *doing* until you came along! There's men after me. That's why me and the other girls lit a shuck out of Coyote Flats so quick."

A fresh wave of tears washed over her eyes, and her muddy cheeks grew a deeper crimson. "And now there'll be *more* because you're trying to take me back *there* to *him*!"

"How do you know someone's after you?" Longarm said amidst her angry sobs, automatically looking around as he remembered the sun flash he'd spied just before encountering her and the other showgirls at the stream.

He didn't doubt that the dwarf's reward had whet the appetites of local bounty hunters, but aside from the man on the stage and the gambler from Kentucky, he had no solid evidence anyone besides himself was on the showgirl's trail.

She sniffed and narrowed her eyes. "Because I *saw* them. We *all* saw them! A couple nights ago, three hard cases were

112

in the saloon where I sang and recited my poetry, and they hung around outside the hotel the next day, staring up at my room."

"In case you hadn't noticed, Coyote Flats is mostly made up of hard cases." Longarm slipped the knot free of her wrists. Making her ride trussed up like a sow for market had been an idle threat. If she tried to run away, he could run her down easily enough. Besides, she had nowhere to go, and no gear to help her get along on this godforsaken prairie. She looked smart enough to realize that. "It *is* in the middle of nowhere, you know, and nice folks tend to clump up in more civilized environs. The rannies in Coyote Flats probably haven't seen a face like yours in a long, dry spell, and they were just drunk and moony."

Sitting up and rubbing her wrists as he untied her ankles, she sniffed, swallowed, and licked her lips. "I've saved some money. Will you let me go if I pay you fifty dollars?"

Longarm sighed, stood, and coiling the lariat over his arm, turned to his horse drawing water from the stream. "Have yourself a long drink. We've got another two hours back to Coyote Flats, and there isn't much water between here and there."

"I suppose you'd let me go if I slept with you. Well, I won't do it. I have principles! I'd rather be dead than ruined by a brute like you!"

He turned to her kneeling in the sand by the stream, her blond hair framing her heart-shaped face. He chuckled to himself, then loosened the horse's saddle cinch. "Well, then, I reckon you're headin' my way. Take a drink and do whatever else you need to do, short of running off. We'll hit the trail again in ten minutes."

Her eyes widened as he swung into the saddle. "Where are you going?"

"Stay here. I'll be right back."

He gigged the horse across the stream, the hooves clattering on the rocks, water splashing up around the paint's knees. When he'd put the mount through the trees on the opposite shore, he looked around for a way up the sandstone ridge, and spotted a game trail. He followed the trail up the ridge at a near forty-five-degree angle, glad to find out the ewe-necked beast was as nimble and had as much bottom as the Mexican hostler had claimed.

The ridge crest was strewn with talus. One spindly pine grew from a split boulder. Longarm drew rein and sat the saddle, scrutinizing the surrounding landscape—first ahead, then behind, careful to let his gaze linger over the rolling, sage-tufted hogbacks and near rimrocks.

He'd been looking west, and was slowly swinging his gaze north for the second time when he stopped and inched his eyes back left. He'd thought he'd spied movement at the brushy lip of a shallow ravine. A thin veil of dust rose. It wasn't as much dust as a horse would lift, but as much as a man on foot, diving for cover, would make.

He held his gaze there, knowing that he was outlined against the sky but not caring. If someone were out here, they already knew he was here, might even have followed him out from town.

On the other hand, the dust might have been kicked up by only a dust devil or a coyote. God knows there were enough of both out here. Best to assume a man had kicked it up, though, and keep one eye peeled on his back trail and one hand on his .44.

The girl might have imagined the dubious interest of the three men in Coyote Flats. Would news of the bounty on her head have traveled so quickly this far off the beaten path? Then again, she might be right, and the three in town might have been waiting for her and the other women to head into the countryside alone. . . .

Longarm cast his gaze down the ridge. The girl stood in the shade of the stream, holding her dress above her knees. She looked so small, young, and forlorn down there, staring up the ridge at him expectantly, that he felt guilty for long-looping her and dragging her back into the firestorm.

What the hell had she been doing in Chugwater anyway? She didn't seem the type that would prostitute herself to a man as obviously reprehensible as the dwarf, even if he was one of the wealthiest owlhoots in the eastern territory. Thinking about that malicious little beast grunting around on her made Longarm's gut roll.

But hell, he'd been wrong about women before. Maybe she didn't care whom she shared her mattress with as long as the sharing paid well. . . .

Longarm had reined the paint back the way he'd come when he glanced once more at the western prairie turning burnt-orange with the west-angling sun, shadows drifting out from the rabbit brush and bunchgrass. Spying movement, he hauled back on the reins and sat tensely, staring west.

Three riders trotted toward him over the crest of a sage-carpeted hogback, spurs and bridle bits flashing in the sunlight. They were little more than copper blurs from this distance, so it was impossible to tell how well they were heeled—whether they were dollar-a-day drovers or bounty hunters—but whoever they were, it was obvious they weren't just enjoying the nice weather.

And they were heading straight for the stream.

Longarm turned toward the girl, but below he saw only the tea-colored water rippling over and between the stones in the streambed. He gigged the horse back down the game trail, across the stream, and through the trees on the other side. He looked around, heart thumping, hoping she hadn't tried to hightail it back to her troupe.

"Miss Ro—!" He stopped as he swung his gaze left.

Amber Rogers stood before a patch of chokecherry shrubs. She wore not a stitch, her pale skin fairly glowing in contrast to the purple shade around her. Her honey-blond hair hung to her shoulders, and her green skirt and white, frilly underwear were sprawled across the branches on her right.

Arms crossed on her chest, she covered her breasts with her hands. Her left foot was perched atop the right, her left knee turned timidly inward. She looked toward Longarm, but rolled her eyes up and down and sideways, as though she couldn't bear to meet his gaze.

"Here I am," she said tensely. "You can take me now, if you'll return me to my troupe after you've had your pleasure."

Longarm ground his molars. "Fool girl, get your clothes on!" The horse tossed its head and sidestepped as Longarm rose up in the saddle, peering through the swishing cottonwoods toward the western prairie beyond, his view blocked by the next rise.

"What?" the girl said in a pinched voice, frowning. "Don't you . . . like—?"

"We got company!" Longarm rasped, holding the paint's reins taut. "Throw your dress on, pronto, and crawl up here!"

Reaching for her underwear, she jerked her head around fearfully. "Damnit, I told you!"

"Forget the underwear," Longarm ordered, keeping one eye peeled on the rise beyond the trees. "Throw that dress on and climb aboard!"

She grabbed the dress and bent forward, stepping into the skirt as her full, round breasts sloped toward the ground. She drew it up her legs to her waist, then shrugged into her blouse. Leaving the blouse unbuttoned, she grabbed her shoes and underwear, and ran barefoot toward Longarm, her breasts jostling between the open flaps of the blouse.

Longarm stretched out his left arm, and she grabbed it. He slung her up onto the horse's rump behind him, then reined the paint sharply right and ground his heels into the horse's flanks.

"Wait!" the girl cried as the paint stretched into a lope, angling toward the trail.

Longarm turned to see the skirt hanging halfway down her long, well-turned legs, flapping like a flag in the wind. Reaching down to pull the garment up, she released her underwear, and the lacy garments flew off like parade bunting before settling in the sage behind them.

"Forget it!" Longarm shouted as he cast his gaze back along the trail. The three riders were nearing the river trees that Longarm and the girl had just left. Now, all three heads turned in Longarm's direction as they reined their mounts to skidding halts, one dun bucking and whinnying, its front hooves clawing at the air before it.

Almost simultaneously, the riders reached for their holsters. Gigging their mounts into gallops toward Longarm and the girl, they raised pistols shoulder high. Smoke puffed around the head of the rider farthest right; then the other two riders snapped off shots a half-wink apart.

All three slugs puffed dirt and gravel well short of the long-striding paint, but Longarm shouted, "Keep your head down!" as he turned forward and slammed his heels once more into the mount's ribs, the paint snorting and surging forward.

"My under—!" She stopped, then shrieked, "Oh, God, they're shooting at us!"

"Hold on," he snapped as the pistols continued popping behind them, sounding little louder than twigs breaking above the thuds of the paint's thundering hooves.

A hundred yards farther down the trail, he glanced over his left shoulder and the girl hunkered down behind him, her open blouse flapping in the wind. The riders were moving toward them steadily, their horses' hooves tearing up gouts of sod and sand. But they didn't seem to be gaining on the paint in spite of the horse having to bear a double load.

That wouldn't last much longer, though. Longarm had a decision to make: stop and fight, or find a way to shake free of the trio tearing up the sod behind him.

He'd try the latter option first.

Continuing to push the mount as hard as he dared, he hoped like hell the horse didn't snap a cannon in a prairie dog hole. He descended a sharp rise and spied a jumble of bleached boulders rising on his left. A few paces farther on, he slowed the paint and turned the horse into a natural corridor in the rocks, pushing through willow and spindly cottonwoods until he was a good twenty yards inside the box canyon.

He lifted his right foot over the horse's neck, dropped to the ground, and turned to the girl. She sat behind the saddle, holding tight to the cantle, dusty breasts exposed between the flaps of her open blouse. Her tussled, seed-flecked hair hung slack down both sides of her face. Her eyes were both frantic and weary.

As she opened her mouth to speak, Longarm cut her off with, "Stay put!"

He used his barlow knife to hack off a slender, leafy cottonwood branch, then ran back out into the trail and crouched to cover his tracks. He glanced up the camelback that he and the girl had just descended, their dust still sifting. No sign yet of the riders, but the clomp of distant hooves was growing louder on the other side of the rise.

When he'd quickly scratched out the prints of the paint's shod hooves for about twenty yards back up the trail, he turned back into the narrow, twisting corridor between walls of strewn boulders and spindly shrubs, and shucked his Winchester from his saddle boot.

The girl shuttled his gaze between him and the trail beyond, her brown eyes bright with fear. She didn't say anything as Longarm levered a shell into the Winchester's breech, jogged back to within six feet of the corridor's mouth, and hunkered down behind a low rock from which a dead cedar twisted.

He could hear the thumps and feel the vibrations of the oncoming riders.

Chapter 14

Longarm doffed his hat and, holding the Winchester low in both hands, peered over the top of the boulder. The thunder of the three horses grew until the loosely bunched trio raced past the mouth of the corridor in a dusty blur, gone before Longarm could make out many details except that the lead rider wore a black leather slouch hat and black vest and that he rode an indistinct dun.

As the hoofbeats dwindled into the distance, Longarm donned his hat and jogged back to where the girl still sat the paint, staring toward him. She'd buttoned her blouse and shoved her dusty hair back behind her ears.

"Are they gone?"

"For now."

"You're a bastard."

"I've been told." Longarm shoved the Winchester into its boot, then grabbed the paint's reins and heaved himself into the saddle. "Don't see any point in you bringin' up the subject, though, since those three doubtless would have found you by now if I hadn't come along and set them on my own trail. *And* they probably would have killed you and the other three women and thrown you all into a ravine . . . minus *your* head, which they'd now be carting back to Chugwater."

He gigged the horse back toward the corridor's opening,

grumbling. "Bastard I may be, but at least I'm willing to take back your entire *body*, mouth and all."

He put the horse back onto the trail, glancing after the three riders who'd disappeared over the next rise, their dust sifting, fresh tracks having stamped the dirt and flattened the short, brown grass. Longarm reined the paint back the way they'd come, and they set off again at a lope up and over the next rise, then swerving off the trail, angling north by northeast cross country.

He traced a circuitous route through the coulees and gullies, walking the horse several times to rest him. An hour after leaving the rocky corridor, he checked the mount down in a shallow coulee bottom from which a lone cottonwood jutted. A dry creek bed curved around the tree, bleached with alkali and spindly tufts of bunchgrass. A grinning coyote skull, as white as the alkali, stared at Longarm and the girl from the cottonwood's forked trunk—probably an old Indian talisman. He hoped it was a lucky sign.

Longarm reached back for the field glasses in his saddlebags. His hand slipped through the slit in the girl's skirt, brushing her inner left thigh.

"Do you mind?" she scolded.

"Sorry."

When she'd moved her leg, he plucked the glasses from the pouch and took a careful gander at the terrain around them. Deciding he'd lost the three riders for now, he gave the binoculars back to the girl with orders to tuck them back into the saddlebags.

"I have to stop soon," she pouted when she'd done as he'd told her. "The horse is chafing my bottom."

"Serves you right for being so quick to shuck out of your underwear," Longarm snorted as he put the paint forward, toward a little burg he'd seen on a map not far from Coyote Flats. Alkali Hollow it was called. He'd avoid Coyote Flats itself, as the bounty hunters would probably look for him and the girl there.

"You're a real chuckle, Mr. Whoever-You-Are," she

grumbled, giving his shoulder blade another halfhearted punch.

"Long," he told her. "Deputy United States Marshal Custis Long. But since you've already shown me your birthday suit, you might as well call me Longarm."

"Did I mention I'm also tired and hungry?"

Longarm sighed as the horse crested the next rise, the sun angling low behind his right shoulder. "I'd forgotten what a pain in the ass showgirls can be."

"I'm an actress."

"Huh?"

"Showgirl connotes hussy. I, on the other hand, am an actress who will be—if you don't get me killed in the next couple of hours—a well-known name very soon."

"If you're so close to bein' as famous at Miss Sarah Bernhardt, how in the hell did you end up at the Dwarf House in Chugwater, Wyoming? Or is that too personal?"

"I know what you're insinuating, but I was never . . . intimate with the dwarf. I was hoodwinked into believing he was something he was not, and that he could do things for me—introduce me to important thespians in Julesburg— that he could not."

Longarm clucked his tongue sarcastically. "And he looks so upstanding."

She slugged him again.

It was near dark when Longarm pulled the horse out of a dry ravine and into a narrow, trash-strewn gap between two stout log buildings. The girl was asleep, her head leaning against his back, her arms wrapped loosely around his waist.

He pulled onto a wide main street carpeted in deep, chalky dust and abutted on both sides by false-fronted business establishments so new they still smelled of pine resin. Stars kindled behind the structures shouldering back against the purple sky.

Having inspected Alkali Hollow from the outlying buttes, he knew that the town was composed of no more than twenty buildings, a good half dozen of them sod or mud-brick shanties. Up the street on his left, lit windows shone before a half-dozen saddle horses standing hang-headed before a hitch rack.

Laughter spilled from the two-story building of vertical, unpainted cottonwood planks—a saloon no doubt, though he couldn't see the shingle from here. It appeared the only watering hole in town. All the other buildings were dark.

No one appeared to be out. Only a couple of buckboard wagons, tongues hanging, were parked along the street from which the day's heat still radiated. A single dog trotted purposefully along the boardwalk to Longarm's right as he booted the horse up the street. When the paint drew abreast of the dog, the cur growled softly but continued past, probably heading for a favorite trash heap.

The main drag bent southward. Just beyond the bend a broad, two-story hip-roofed building stood, a couple of windows lit. The shingle jutting into the street announced simply HOTEL.

Longarm drew the paint up to the hitch rack and dismounted, holding the slumbering girl with one hand. Gently, he shook her. She grumbled and muttered, then lifted her head suddenly, giving a soft, startled cry.

"It's all right," Longarm said, gently pulling her out of the saddle. "We're there."

"Where's there?" she muttered as she stood beside him, shoving her hair back from her eyes and looking around groggily.

"It ain't Denver. Come on—we'll get us a room."

When he'd grabbed his rifle and war bag and had tied the paint's reins to the hitch rack, he mounted the stoop and walked through the hotel's front door. Inside the dimly lit front room, at the rear of which a timber staircase rose into shadows, a burly gent sat behind a high plank desk on the right. A round-faced Indian woman with a scabbed lower lip, bruised right eye, and long, braided hair sat in a rough-hewn rocking chair to the left, sewing with thread and needle what appeared to be a doeskin skirt.

"Help you?" the burly man said, shoving aside his yellowed newspaper and scrutinizing Longarm and the girl who shuffled wearily in behind him.

The man's greasy, sandy hair hung to his shoulders from a soiled derby trimmed with a ratty eagle feather. A clock ticked on the wall behind the desk.

"A room," Longarm said.

Voices rose behind the burly man, and Longarm shuttled his gaze to a doorway covered with a flour-sack curtain. He set his war bag on the desk, walked over to the curtain, slowly slid it aside with the back of his right hand, and peered into a small saloon area lit by a few smoky lamps and candles.

The light was reflected in the cracked mirror of the back bar on the room's far side. Six or seven round tables were haphazardly arranged about the earthen floor. Three men sat at one table in the middle of the room—dusty, sweaty hombres in rough trail garb and sporting revolvers in holsters thonged on their thighs. Each held playing cards in his hand, and tobacco smoke wafted over the table.

The gent with his back to Longarm wore a cracked bullhide vest. A black leather hat sat on the chair beside him. The hide-wrapped handle of a bowie knife poked up from under his shirt collar behind his neck.

Longarm cursed under his breath, his right hand squeezing the Winchester's forestock.

The man on the far left glanced at Longarm, glanced away, then looked back and held his gaze on the stranger peering through the curtain. The other two followed his gaze, the hombre with his back to Longarm hipping around and making his chair squawk as though it were about to break.

"Just gonna stand there and stare, mister?" said the man with the black hat around the wheat-paper quirley in his teeth. "Or you want us to deal you in?"

Longarm held his gaze. Were these the three who'd been after him? Most likely, but he couldn't be sure. Since they weren't making a play, he wouldn't either.

"Some other time," he said, and let the curtain fall back into place.

He turned to the burly gent sitting on a high stool behind the desk and regarding him expectantly. The Indian woman regarded Longarm curiously over the dress she was sewing in her lap while she rocked.

"They staying here?" Longarm said, hooking his thumb toward the curtain.

"That's right. Rode in about twenty minutes before you."

Longarm felt the girl's eyes on him as he said, "About that room . . ."

The burly gent turned and grabbed a key off a hook, dropped it on the desk, and turned the register book toward Longarm, opening it and dipping a pen in the inkwell beside it. "Room Seven's got a double bed."

Longarm picked up the pen. "Which room is across from Seven?"

"Nine."

"I'll take that one too." He cocked an eyebrow at the burly gent. "That's our official room, if you get my drift."

The burly gent hiked a shoulder, turned, grabbed another key, and plopped it down on the book.

"We'll stay in Seven though I'm signing for Nine. Understand?"

"Mister, I understand Chinese as long as said Chinese plops cash down on my desk here . . . for both rooms."

Longarm set two silver dollars on the counter. The man looked down at them, then peered up at the lawman from beneath his bunched brows.

"Bring up a couple steaks with all the surroundings, a bottle of your best whiskey, and a jug of water. Set them on the floor outside Room Nine. There a stable in town?"

"Got my own out back."

"There's a paint on the street. Stable him. Rub him down good, and grain him. I'd like some women's underwear, around her size"—he canted his head at Amber—"brought up when you bring the food. Bring her a jacket too."

Longarm tossed down another dollar. "Will that cover it?"

The burly gent smiled and glanced at the Indian woman, who'd stopped rocking behind Longarm. "I reckon. . ."

Longarm grabbed both keys off the desk, tossed his saddlebags over his shoulder, and glanced at the girl. She regarded him edgily.

Longarm smiled and stepped aside to let her pass toward the stairs. "Well, honey, it's been a long ride. . . ."

Amber glanced at the curtained doorway, then moved across the room and started up the stairs. Longarm followed her up to the second story, which was dark and musty. At Room Seven, he set his saddlebags on the floor, turned the key in the lock, and opened the door. Warm, trapped air flowed over him as he tossed the saddlebags on the bed and fumbled to light a hurricane lantern on the dresser.

When the wick caught, spreading a wan glow over the brass-framed bed sagging in the middle and covered with an Indian blanket, he said, "Home sweet home."

She came in, closed the door, and crossed her arms on her chest. "They're here, aren't they?"

Still holding the Winchester in one hand, Longarm pried open the room's sole window. "If so, they're sneaky bastards."

"How did that happen?" Her voice grew steadily louder and shriller. "I thought you were a deputy United States marshal known far and wide as Longarm because you're so *goddamn good at your job!*"

"*Shhh!* If that's them down there, we want them to think we're in *there.*"

Longarm opened the door and poked his head out, listening. Hearing nothing, he walked to the other door, opened it, stepped inside, and lit the lamp on the washstand.

Leaving the lamp aglow, he walked out, locked the door, dropped the key in his pocket, and returned to Room Seven, in which the girl lay sprawled facedown on the bed. He heard her sobbing softly as he propped his hat in front of the lamp, shielding the glow from the door.

Later, when a single set of light footsteps—the Indian woman's probably—tapped on the stairs and in the hall, pausing nearby before drifting back down the stairs, Longarm cracked the door and peeked out. A whiskey bottle, a stone water jug, and two plates draped with oilcloth sat before the door to Room Nine. Beside them lay a lumpy burlap sack.

Longarm retrieved both plates and the sack, handing one plate and the unmentionables to the girl.

"I'm not hungry," she said snootily, setting the plate on the washstand beside the bed.

"Eat."

"I'm not hungry."

"Suit yourself."

When he'd retrieved the whiskey bottle—his rye bottle was nearly empty—and the water jug, and locked their door, he sat in a spool-back chair before the door, boots propped on the bed frame. The steak was a tad overdone and the beans were chewy, but the boiled potatoes buried in gravy and the sourdough bun slathered in butter were just right, and Longarm's plate was clean in five minutes.

As he set the plate on the floor and plucked the cork from the bottle, he glanced to his left and saw that Amber had propped her plate on her thighs, and was going to work on the food like a range rider after nine hours of fence-stretching.

Longarm chuckled to himself and raised the bottle. "Drink?"

Chewing, she glanced at him, then grabbed a water glass off the washstand and extended it toward him. He half-filled the glass, then leaned back in his chair. He tossed back a long drink, then snagged his Winchester off the bed and stared at the door.

If the three men downstairs were the men who'd triggered lead after him and the girl—and he had to believe they were—there'd be trouble soon.

Chapter 15

After the steak, Longarm wanted a cigar in the worst way. The smoke might give him and the girl away, however, so he settled for another long pull from the bottle and continued staring at the door, his rifle angled across his thighs, boots propped on the bedpost.

Behind him, Amber dropped her fork on the clay plate and belched softly. Longarm glanced over his left shoulder as she set the plate, which she'd cleaned nearly as well as he'd cleaned his, on the washstand and picked up her whiskey glass.

"Get enough, or you want me to have 'em send up the cow?"

She smirked. "I've always had a hearty appetite. Miss Taylor said I could put on a few pounds."

"You keep eating like that, you're gonna need a hollow leg."

He heard her sip from her glass. "We don't know each other well enough for you to be talking to me that way. Besides, aren't you supposed to act professional? There you sit, with your feet up, guzzling whiskey while you're supposed to be protecting me."

"I protect better when I'm half stewed. Keep your voice down."

"I'm gonna wash up," she whispered. The bedsprings squawked and he felt the air in the stale room move as she got up off the bed. "Don't look."

Longarm snorted as he took another swig of whiskey. "Anything I haven't seen so far?"

She didn't respond to that. Her clothes rustled and her bare feet tapped the floor behind him. Water splashed into a bowl. He rolled his eyes left. She stood before the washstand, her hands moving across her chest. He couldn't see her clearly from this angle, but he could see that she was naked. He felt a twitch down low, took another swig from the bottle, and stared at the door.

"If you're trying to bribe me again," he growled, "it won't work."

The crackle of soap and water stopped suddenly. "Did you peek?"

"I'm a professional."

The crackle continued as her arms resumed moving across her chest and belly. "I assure you my intention is merely to get some trail dust off. I realize now that the only way to ever be free is to have Mr. Turley put away for good . . . or hanged."

"So that's his name."

"He's a vile little man. I was made a fool, and now he's trying to kill me." She paused. Longarm could feel her eyes on him. "And he probably will, but I'll go down with a fight, damnit!"

"Shhh."

"What is it?" she whispered.

Longarm held up a hand, listening. Voices sounded downstairs. Boots pounded the stairs—heavy, tired footsteps. Spurs chinged.

A drunken voice echoed in the stairwell. "I sure never expected you to have that jack. Damn you, Claw! You got some luck, you know that?"

"The luck of the stupid," said another, deeper voice, chuckling.

"Fuck you, Greene. I'm that one that done *taught* you how to play stud."

The men continued bantering as the footsteps grew louder.

Longarm glanced at the girl standing wet and naked behind him, squeezing her breasts in her hands, and motioned her under the bed. She grabbed a towel and, quickly wrapping it around herself, got down on her hands and knees and scrambled out of sight beneath the sagging mattress and overhanging quilt.

Breathing shallowly, Longarm gained his feet.

The floorboards vibrated as, out in the hall, the three men sauntered toward Longarm's room. The drink-thick banter resonated off the walls.

Longarm pressed his back against the wall left of the door and held the Winchester at port, thumbing back the hammer and snugging his finger against the trigger. He followed the men by their voices and footsteps, until they were directly between his door and the door of Room Nine.

The smell of sweaty, dusty bodies, leather, liquor, and horses tainted the air.

Longarm stiffened, held his breath, waiting.

But the men didn't stop. Their boots continued thumping along the hall, growing slightly quieter until the pounding was replaced by soft scuffs and scrapes. A minute later, the banter abated. The men bade each other gruff good-nights as keys clanked in locks. One man swatted another with his hat, chuckling, and then two doors barked shut.

Longarm kept his back pressed against the wall, frowning. He'd be damned.

Something rustled beneath the bed. The girl whispered, "Are they gone?"

Longarm kept his ears pricked, his finger on the Winchester's trigger. "Sounds like."

"Maybe they're not the three who were after us."

"I reckon you might be right."

"Should I stay down here?"

"Up to you." Longarm picked up his whiskey bottle, took another pull, then lay down on the bed and crossed his ankles. The girl's head rose from the floor just beyond his dusty boots. She twisted her face around until her eyes met his.

"Close your eyes."

"How am I supposed to protect you with my eyes closed?"

"Just close them, will you?" she snapped.

When he'd closed his eyes, he heard her bare feet pad around to his left, and she resumed washing, her movements more harried now. She brushed her hair, dressed, and then she crawled into bed to his right, tossing back all the covers but only covering herself with the sheet.

"Can I open my eyes?"

"Yes, but stay over there."

Longarm chuckled. He opened his eyes, feeling the fatigue from the long ride in the hot sun wash over him, but keeping his ears pricked for sound.

He glanced to his left. Amber lay curled on the far side of the bed, turned away from him, her taut rump jutting toward him. Her damp hair was sprayed across her pillow.

Her voice rose softly. "It was ghastly, what the dwarf did to that poor man."

"How'd you come to see it?"

"I was going to Mr. Turley's office to tell him I felt I had no future there in the Dwarf House. He'd assured me that agents from Denver, Julesburg, and Leadville visited all the time, but in the three weeks I was there, I never saw anyone who looked remotely like an agent. Army scouts and prospectors and drovers, sure, but no agents."

She rolled onto her back and stared up at the ceiling. "Anyway, as I approached the office, I heard the gunshot. One of his men came out, and through the open door I saw the mayor of Chugwater lying on the floor near Mr. Turley's desk."

She paused, her eyes moving around in their sockets, as if she were watching the scene played out on the wainscoted ceiling above.

"As the poor man lay bleeding on the floor, he looked directly into my eyes and mouthed, 'Help me.' It was awful. The dwarf was laughing. He saw me standing there in the hall, and he called me in, said I'd see something I'd never forget. I turned and ran back to my room. I lit out with Miss Taylor two days later. To think that that *vile* little man had invited me there to charm me. He actually thought I'd be his . . . whore!"

She turned and, sobbing, threw her arms around Longarm's neck, pressing her soft body against his as she stared into his eyes beseechingly. "You won't let him kill me, will you?"

She looked so young and vulnerable suddenly that Longarm lifted his hands to her smooth, slightly sunburned face, and smoothed her hair back from her eyes. "He's not gonna kill you, Miss Rogers. I guarantee you that."

She smiled and narrowed her eyes like a cat, soothed, enjoying his caress. Her full lips parted slightly, and she pushed her face toward him, her damp eyes closing, her lips touching his. As she kissed him, her breasts pressed against his ribs, and she crooked her left leg over his thigh, her knee riding up close to his crotch.

Her full lips parted, seeming to swell. "You make me feel . . . safe—"

Hearing the faintest sound from the hall, and seeing a shadow move underneath the door, Longarm sprang up and to the left, throwing the girl flat against the bed. Her eyes and mouth snapped wide, and she gave a clipped scream as Longarm threw himself on top of her. Snaking his arms beneath her, he rolled off the far side of the bed, taking her with him to the floor.

Longarm's back hit the puncheons with a loud thud, the girl sprawled on top of him. At the same time, a deafening *BOOM!* filled the room like a cannon blast. Amber yowled as, with the back of his left arm, Longarm shoved her down against the wall and rose to his knees, clawing his .44 from the cross-draw holster on his left hip.

The door flew wide, spewing smoke and splinters and with a pumpkin-sized hole in its middle, flames nibbling at the edges of the hole, like a giant cigarette burn on paper.

Two men bolted into the room, one behind the other—the black-hatted man from downstairs wielding a smoking double-barreled shotgun, and one of his compadres raising a stout, octagonal-barreled Spencer to his left shoulder.

Both men jerked their heads around, both sets of eyes finding Longarm kneeling on the far side of the bed at the same time. The black-hatted gent's shotgun came down first. Longarm, who hadn't yet aimed his double-action Colt, ducked as the barn-blaster's right barrel flashed and roared.

It rocked the entire room, tearing yellow corn shucks from the mattress over Longarm's head and throwing them back against the wall above the cowering girl.

Longarm gritted his teeth as the Spencer spoke, sounding little louder than a bone breaking after the shotgun's ear-hammering report. The girl screamed as the slug barked into the wall behind Longarm's right shoulder.

Longarm jerked his head up and extended the gun across the bed. As the man with the Spencer ejected the spent casing, the black-hatted man tossed the shotgun onto the bed.

As the gut-shredder bounced off the mattress, Longarm squeezed the Colt's trigger. The black-hatted gent had been clawing his Colt Navy from his low-slung holster when Longarm's round careened through his breast plate, deftly cleaving the one-inch gap between his black vest lapels and sending him staggering and grunting back toward the burning door.

As the black-hatted gent screamed and triggered a .44 bullet into the floor at his stumbling feet, Longarm slid the Colt right and fired. His round slid for about six inches along the breech of the Spencer, which the second gent had snugged up to his left cheek. The man screamed as the sparking bullet ripped through his mouth and out the side of his head just below his right ear, spraying blood. His head whipped to one side and he ricocheted a round off the bed's left rear post and into the dresser mirror with a crash of breaking glass.

The girl cried as, somewhere behind Longarm—in the next room?—a rifle boomed twice. Longarm heard the shots rip through the wall behind him, spraying pine slivers and buzzing around his ears before one cracked the porcelain washbowl and the other barked into the far wall.

Meanwhile, the gent he'd shot in the mouth got his feet beneath him, shook his head like a wet dog, and gritting his bloody teeth, rammed a fresh shell into his Spencer's chamber and swung the barrel toward Longarm.

Longarm triggered a shot through his chest.

As he wheeled, screaming and triggering a slug into the ceiling, two more shots popped through the wall behind Longarm, the girl complaining with each shot as she kicked at the floorboards, her head in her arms.

Longarm glanced right. The black-hatted gent knelt in front of the smoking door—the fire had gone out—and was raising his Colt in his right hand. Longarm drilled another shot through the man's gut.

As the man's .44 dropped in his hand and he knelt there, throwing his head back and screaming like a gut-shot coyote, Longarm flung himself forward. He rolled off the bed, grabbing his Winchester, and dropped to a knee on the bed's far side.

He rammed a fresh shell in the breech and winced as another hole appeared in the wall before him and ripped off a seven-inch sliver of pine slat before curling the air over Longarm's head.

Longarm triggered the Winchester, levered a fresh shell, fired again and again until he'd stitched eight holes into the same broad group the shooter had fired on the other side.

A muffled voice rose. *"Ahhhhh!"* Boots beat a raucous rhythm against the floorboards in the room beyond, spurs chinging like loose change in a pocket. There was the clash of a breaking window and the man's yell growing thinner before it died.

Automatically, Longarm began thumbing fresh shells into his rifle's loading door while he swung his head around the smoky room rife with the smell of charred wood and cordite. One of the bushwhackers was piled up in a bloody pool on the room's far side. The man who'd been wearing the black hat still knelt before the smoking door, arms crossed on his belly, his head bowed as if in prayer.

"Stay where you are," Longarm told the girl as he stood

and, thumbing the last shell through the Winchester's loading door, strode toward the open doorway.

The belly-shot hombre lifted his head, his features taut with pain, his rheumy eyes hard. His voice was raspy. "I reckon you killed me . . . Longarm."

Longarm stopped. "You have the advantage here, pard."

"Nails Willie. Wichita, Kansas." The man winced and shook as if chilled, blood welling out from between his crossed arms. "Five years ago. With the money for her head . . . I was sorta plannin' on goin' straight."

"Damn, Nails," Longarm said, stepping through the doorway while holding the Winchester straight up and down, "you got close."

Longarm heard the thump of Nails's head hitting the floor behind him as he stepped into the hall, swinging his head from left to right, looking around for more trouble. Smelling a rotten fish, he sidestepped toward the stairwell in the half-darkness ahead, the wall at the top of the stairs lit by lamplight bleeding up from below.

The hall was silent. So was the rest of the hotel. Not even a dog barked on the street.

Two feet from the stairwell, Longarm pressed his right shoulder against the wall. He continued forward, stopped at the intersection of the second-story wall and the stairs dropping into the wan lamplight below.

He listened.

Still hearing nothing, he edged his left eye around the corner, glancing down the stairs. The burly hotel owner stood halfway up the staircase. He had a look of extreme concentration on his fleshy, bearded face as he aimed a long, double-barreled shotgun in both hands toward the left newel post at the top of the stairs.

The man's eyes snapped wide as they slid toward Longarm. Longarm ducked back behind the wall. A quarter second later, the shotgun boomed, ripping a large chunk out of the wall corner and flinging it across the hall.

Longarm stepped into the stairwell, snugging the Winchester's butt against his shoulder and squeezing the trigger.

The rifle barked and jerked, and the burly barman's head snapped back with the force of the slug drilled between his eyes. He spread his arms as though they were wings, dropping the barn-blaster over the railing and falling straight back onto the steps with a thunderous crack before turning and rolling to the bottom.

Longarm ejected the spent, smoking shell and stared down the stairwell as the cartridge clattered onto the floor behind him.

Below, the Indian woman stepped out from behind the desk and stood over the dead man—her husband, Longarm assumed. She looked up at Longarm, the swollen eye and puffy lip looking dark against her round, russet face.

"He always been greedy." She looked down at the burly man bleeding out at the base of the stairs, and prodded his shoulder twice with her slippered foot. Returning her gaze to Longarm, she offered a chip-toothed grin. "You got him good."

He lowered the rifle to his side. "You got a town marshal, sheriff, or somethin' like that?"

"Constable Bergie rides over once a week from Coyote Flats."

Longarm cursed and frowned down at the dead man at the base of the stairs. "I'll wire him when I get a chance. I'll haul these cadavers outside, find someone to bury 'em in the morning." He nodded politely. "Sorry about your . . . loss."

She grinned at him again, showing even more teeth. She jerked her head to indicate the girl in the room to Longarm's right, and her tea-colored eyes gave him the quick twice-over. "She's too skinny for you. You stay here and help me run this place, huh?"

Longarm grinned. "We'd have some fun, wouldn't we?" He winked, turned, and headed back to his room.

Chapter 16

Longarm and the Indian woman hauled all the bodies out of the hotel and into the stable in the backyard. They had to look hard for the man who'd fired from the room next to Longarm's and the girl's, for when he'd fallen out the window, he'd rolled into a brushy gully abutting the hotel.

When they finally found him, he was still alive.

The Indian woman told Longarm he might as well finish the man with his sidearm, as there was no doctor within thirty-five miles, and it was clear his neck was broken anyway. When Longarm explained that such a maneuver, while practical, wasn't in the lawman's book of proper etiquette, she offered to strangle the gent with her apron.

But the whole issue was soon moot. Hearing the last breath rattle up from the man's throat as they carried him out of the ravine, Longarm and the Indian woman swerved toward the stable, where they piled the gent's body with the other three, including the Indian woman's deceased but unlamented common-law husband.

Longarm had learned over the past hour that the burly hotel proprietor's name was Ferdinand. He'd purchased the Indian woman for a sack of potatoes from a shotgun rancher seventeen miles south of Alkali Hollow. Ferdinand had beaten her daily whether she'd deserved it or not. That's why she wasn't sorry to see him kick out with a shovel, but wondered aloud who was going to finish digging the new privy pit.

Longarm allowed he didn't know, but he'd help her clean up the blood inside the hotel. She said she'd clean tomorrow, and they parted company around midnight, Longarm returning to Room Seven, where Amber sat up in the bed, sound asleep with her chin on her chest, her back against the headboard, his Winchester resting across her thighs. He gently removed the gun from her hands, and she sagged sideways onto the bed, out like a blown lamp.

It didn't take long for Longarm to drift off as well, listening even in his sleep for sounds of more trouble. But when he opened his eyes again, yellow morning light reflected off the cottonwood branches out the room's single window, and the breeze blew cool and fresh, faintly tinged with the smell of alkali and clover.

Amber slept snugged beside him, more on his side of the bed than hers but facing the window, the shotgun-shredded quilt drawn up taut to her chin. Her warm butt was rammed against his left hip.

Before his member stirred—he had no time for "trifling with the girl," as Billy Vail would call it, as he had only a day and a half to get the girl back to Jim Friendly before the dwarf was freed—he threw the covers back, sat up in bed, and grabbed a half-smoked cheroot from the washstand.

"Custis?" the girl said, her voice thick with sleep.

He'd lit the cheroot and was about to take a morning bracer from his rye bottle.

"Up and at 'em, girl—we're burnin' daylight."

He lifted the bottle and bubbled it twice, swishing the liquor around in his mouth before swallowing it.

She moved a leg under the quilt, but made no effort to rise. "How're we gonna get into Chugwater? I mean, Mr. Turley has a whole passel of gunmen on his roll. He'll have every entrance to the town covered."

While she'd spoken, horse hooves thudded and a wagon clattered outside the window. "Hold up there, gents," a man said, the voice just audible above the fluttering cottonwood leaves.

Vaguely curious about what was happening on the street below, Longarm strolled toward the window, barefoot but otherwise fully dressed, avoiding the blood on the floor. The cigar drooped from his lips while he carried the rye bottle by its neck down low against his thigh.

It was a good question. How were they going to get into Chugwater without being shot like ducks on a millpond? Longarm had asked himself that very question several times, but hadn't yet come up with an answer.

He didn't have time to cable Billy Vail for help.

Out the window, a somnolent voice rose in prayer: "Our Father which art in Heaven, hallowed be Thy name . . ."

Longarm stepped up to the window and, blinking against the morning light flashing silver off the cottonwoods, looked out. On the street to his far left, at the mouth of the ravine from which he and the Indian woman had pulled the last gent's body, a beat-up buckboard stood behind two mismatched horses.

The men Longarm had shot lay heaped in the box, limbs akimbo. One body lay with his head near the box's open tailgate, one stiff arm poking straight out from the end, open eyes glaring.

Around the box stood three ratty-garbed, unshaven townsmen, the Indian woman—whose name Longarm hadn't learned—wearing the same dress and apron she'd worn last night, and a severe-looking cuss in a white shirt with sleeve garters, a dark-blue vest, and a minister's collar. The preacher stood on the far side of the wagon, holding his bullet-crowned black hat across his heart as he recited, ". . . on Earth as it is Heaven. Give us this day our daily bread. And forgive us our trespasses, as we forgive them that trespass—"

The preacher stopped and turned to a shaggy, burr-infested dog that had jumped up on the wagon's open tailgate and was sniffing around the dead man at the end.

"Get *a-way*, you foul creature!" the preacher shouted, swatting at the dog with his hat.

The dog yipped as it jumped off the tailgate and hit the dirt running.

"That's Avery Kermit's mongrel," said the man standing nearest the preacher as he slipped an old Schofield revolver from his holster.

He aimed at the fleeing dog and snapped off a shot. The slug blew up dust a foot behind the dog's striding back legs with a whining twang. The dog yowled fearfully and disappeared into a gap between business buildings on the other side of the street.

When the shooter had holstered his pistol and crossed his hands before the buckle of his cartridge belt once more, the preacher continued.

Longarm didn't hear the rest of the prayer, however. He stared at the minister, deep in thought. When the preacher had donned his hat and stepped back as the townsmen ushered the wagon up the street, the Indian woman walking about ten feet behind the tailgate, Longarm turned to Amber.

She lay on the bed, frowning up at him skeptically, awaiting an answer to her question about how they were going to make it into Chugwater alive.

Longarm puffed the cigar, then took another swig of the rye. "Oh, ye of little faith." He grinned. "Didn't I tell you I was a professional?"

An hour later, Longarm and Amber were riding through a broad valley between sandstone rimrocks painted lime green and aquamarine by the climbing morning sun, in the leather-seated, red-wheeled buggy Longarm had bought from Alkali Hollow's Presbyterian minister, Brother John Bernard Frye.

Not only had he procured the minister's buggy, he'd also bought the minister's hat, vest, and collar, all of which he now wore. Beside him on the comfortable cowhide seat, Amber Rogers wore a traveling outfit that had belonged to the minister's wife, who, it had fortuitously turned out, was only about one size larger than Amber.

The prim, deep-purple skirt with ruffled white blouse and purple, laced-edged jacket hung slightly on the girl's willowy, deep-busted frame, but as long as she remained seated in the buggy, no one would know the attire had been borrowed from a larger woman old enough to be her grandmother. The felt box hat and net veil obscured her features enough that no one who didn't scrutinize her would ever recognize her as the showgirl heading for Chugwater to rat out the infamous dwarf. She looked like a pretty, young minister's wife on the trail with her pious betrothed to spread the Word of the Lord, according to the story Longarm had made up in case anyone asked, to the heathens down Cheyenne way.

"I don't see how men of the cloth can wear these collars," Longarm said, stretching his neck to loosen the tight paper band around his neck. "I feel like a rooster some old lady's wringin' for the stew pot."

She stared up at him from beneath her vail, hands in her lap. "I think you look right handsome as a minister."

"That's cause *your* duds aren't strangling *you.*"

She slapped his arm. "Quit messin' with it. You're gonna tear it, and you won't look like a minister anymore."

Longarm dropped his hand, swallowed hard to get the spit down his pinched throat. "You're bossy."

She stared out the off-side of the buggy, at the Laramie Mountains rising blue and spruce-green and striped with cloud shadows in the west. "Custis, did you grow up in a God-fearing house?"

"I reckon we were about as God-fearing as any." He turned to her. "You?"

She shook her head and sucked in her cheeks. "My pa didn't have time for such nonsense after Ma died. We lived on a farm in Iowa. He was a harsh man, worked me and my brothers from sunup to sundown. That's why I ran off with a traveling show three years ago, and took up the entertainer's life." She turned toward him, her light-brown eyes saucy. "I say *entertainer*. That don't mean *whore.* Some think they're one and the same."

"You already set me straight on that."

"Maybe you'll hear me sing sometime, or recite my poetry. Like I say, I ain't a doxie"—she leaned toward Longarm, intimately touched her left shoulder to his right one—"but I do enjoy the look the men acquire when they hear me recite the rhymes of Lord Byron."

Longarm chuckled. He had no doubt that, with her looks, she could have filled a dance hall if she only read the dictionary. He remembered a pretty whore in Denver who once read the Christmas story in the Black Cat Saloon. While the girl read those Bible verses to the half-stewed drovers and miners down from the hills, you could have heard a pin drop anywhere in town.

"Longarm?" she asked as he dug a half-smoked cheroot from his shirt pocket. "You know what my real name is?"

Longarm feined surprise as he struck a match to life on his thumbnail. "It ain't Amber Rogers?"

"Trudy Hill." She sucked her cheeks again and waited for his reaction.

"Pleased to meet you all over again, Trudy."

"Don't call me Trudy." She looked away again. "That life's behind me now. I just felt like telling you my real name . . . in case I died or something. So you could cable my pa and brothers in Davenport."

"You're not gonna die." Longarm wrapped his right arm around her shoulders and pressed her to him briefly. "You're gonna testify against the dwarf, then light out once more for fame and fortune."

"Will you come and hear me sing?"

"Hell, if you're anywhere near Denver, wild horses wouldn't keep me away." He stretched his neck again, as the paper collar had dug into his three-day growth of beard, pinching his wind and making the beard stubble itch. "If I don't suffocate, that is. Or if my boss doesn't kill me for shelling out a hundred dollars of Uncle's Sam lucre for these duds and rig that aren't worth half that much."

He'd hired a boy to return the paint horse to the Mexican hostler at the livery barn in Coyote Flats. Unfortunately, Alkali Hollow hadn't had a telegraph office, so Longarm hadn't been able to wire an update to Billie or to Jim

Friendly in Chugwater. No doubt the chief marshal was storming around his office, calling Longarm every name he'd ever called him while making up a few more.

Jim was probably just plain nervous. Longarm's deadline for getting the girl back to Chugwater was noon tomorrow.

"It was for a good cause," the girl reminded Longarm with an edgy pitch to her voice as he stared off down the trail from behind her vale.

"Billie takes some convincing."

They rode over a couple of rises, the sun beating down on the buggie's canopy and burnishing the dust kicked up by the black's hooves. Longarm kept a sharp eye on their back trail and on the rolling, sage-tufted hills around them, happy to have seen nothing more out of the ordinary than jack-rabbits, a couple of coyotes, and two golden eagles picking at a deer carcass on a distant knoll. So far, two rattlers had slithered across the trail in front of the preacher's black horse, who'd shaken his head at them with annoyance.

"Custis, I just want you to know that I wouldn't have got-ten near as friendly last night if I hadn't drank all that whiskey." Her body jerking sharply when the rig's front left tire hit a rock, she glanced up at him demurely, biting her lower lip. "Just wanted to make sure you didn't think I was a loose woman. 'Cause some men . . ."

"I know," Longarm grumbled, puffing the cigar in his teeth, holding the ribbons loose in his gloved hands. "Some men mistake showgirls for whores."

"And if I should overimbibe again on account of my nerves"—turning toward him again, she lifted her veil to give him a gently admonishing look, her smooth cheeks col-oring slightly—"I hope you wouldn't take advantage."

Longarm faked a hurt expression. "I done told you, Miss Amber . . ."

"I know," she grumbled, pursing lips at him again, one eye crossing slightly, "you're a professional."

Longarm laughed and shook the ribbons over the horse's sweat-damp back, and they shot around a hill shoulder. Since it was made for considerably less rugged terrain closer

143

to town, the buggy tilted downhill so steeply that the left front and rear wheels rose a dangerous six inches off the ground before the grade gentled, and they were headed for the next valley.

Following the rough map the minister had sketched for them, delineating a short if rugged route to Chugwater, they continued up and down the hogbacks, angling ever closer toward the Laramie Mountains on the right.

They wound around rimrocks and crossed several creeks, Longarm having to half-carry the buggy over a couple of the especially deep watercourses. The trail thinned out to little more than an antelope trail in places, tougher even to follow when the sun dipped behind the jagged western peaks.

"Shouldn't we stop?" Amber asked when the stars closed down like candlelit Christmas ornaments.

"I want to get as far as we can, so we have a short trip tomorrow. If we're not in Chugwater by noon, Jim's gonna have to turn the dwarf back out on society."

"What is it?" Amber asked as Longarm leaned forward to squint into the darkness over the horse's head.

About fifty yards away, between a copse of trees and a low butte, shadows moved. "I don't know." Longarm reached under the seat for his Winchester and pulled back on the reins.

As the shadows jostled, growing larger, hooves clomped, growing louder.

Amber gasped and dug her fingers into Longarm's left forearm as someone shouted, "Hold it right there!"

Chapter 17

As Amber dug her fingers into his arm, Longarm stopped the black in the narrow trail curving ahead like pale bunting in the darkness, and set the Winchester across his knees.

"Who goes there?" a young man's brittle voice yelled to his right, above the thud of hooves and the crackling brush in the aspen copse.

Resisting the temptation to jack a round into the Winchester's chamber, Longarm left the rifle across his knees and kept his hands on the black's reins. Shadows moved toward him from ahead and right. Starlight winked off gunmetal.

"Easy, brothers," Longarm called, ignoring Amber's long fingernails digging through his coat sleeve. "It's the Reverend and Mrs. Angus Peabody here, two weary night travelers meaning no harm to anyone, just followin' the trail to Cheyenne by way of Chugwater. We hope you're as God-fearin' as we are and will let us pass unharassed. In return, we'll put in a good word for you with the guardian at the Pearly Gates."

Longarm hadn't been around enough preachers lately to know how they talked, so he'd had to make it up, inwardly wincing and ready to snap the Winchester up if the night riders didn't buy it. The muscles in the back of his neck slackened, however, when the rider moving up on his right materialized from the brush and, giving Longarm and the girl the quick twice-over by starlight, turned toward the two men closing from up trail, exclaiming, "Hey, Pa, it's a sky pilot!"

Ahead, one of the riders paused near the black while the other—a big, portly gent in stockman's garb and with an old saddle gun snugged against his broad right thigh—rode up on Longarm's left. The big man leaned out from his saddle, making the leather squeak, as he inspected Longarm and the girl huddled against him and still trying to claw through the flesh in his right forearm.

"Well, I'll be jigged!" the man said. "Hello, Reverend!"

Longarm offered his best beatific grin. "Howdy, brother. Just the Reverend and Mrs. Peabody here. If we're trespassin' on private land, we do apologize. We're following a map drawn by the good Brother Frye from up at Alkali Hollow, who directed us via the shortest route possible to Cheyenne, where a new church is awaiting our services—those of the Missus Peabody and myself, that is."

"Well, it is private land, Reverend—my land, for a fact. Jack Gowdy's my name and these are my boys, Kenny and Kendal. We've been having problems with long-loopers of late, and that's why we're so quick to inquire of night travelers. I do apologize if we startled you and the missus."

Gowdy removed his hat, his mouth forming a toothless oval as he smiled reassuringly at Amber. He was round-faced and nearly bald, with tufts of hair jutting from his ears and broad nostrils, and his round-rimmed glasses winked in the starlight. He wore a beard but no mustache.

"We understand, Brother Gowdy," Longarm said with a polite nod. "And we'll waylay your patrol no longer . . ." Longarm raised his hands, ready to shake the leather ribbons over the black, until Gowdy shook his head, frowning.

"Pshaw, Reverend! You can't travel no more tonight. Why, it's dark as pitch, and the trail worsens a whole heap at the Devil's Backbone dead ahead. Dang near unpassable by night even on horseback, let alone in that light rig of yourn."

146

Longarm opened his mouth to speak, but Gowdy cut him off.

"We insist you follow us back to the home place for some hot vittles and a soft bed. We're God-fearin' folk ourselves, and it's right seldom we get the privilege of sheltering *anyone*, let alone a couple of such pious distinction. Besides, if Ma knew I let a man of the cloth pass without stoppin' at the cabin to say a few words over her table, she'd tar and feather my fat ole carcass and run me into the Laramies on a long, greased pole!" Gowdy slapped his thigh and guffawed, glancing at his beefy sons. "Won't she, boys?"

The boys—the one nearest the buggy being short and skinny while the other was nearly as large as their old man—forced a chuckle.

"Besides," Gowdy said, "you're just in time for supper. We always eat late, as me and Kendal and Kenny make a swing around the range at sunset. That's when we've been hit hardest by long-loopers."

Longarm wanted to keep moving at least as far as the Devil's Backbone, which the preacher had marked on the map as well as warned him about, but he knew Amber was tired and would rather sleep with a roof over her head. So after the required polite hesitation, assuring Gowdy that the Reverend and Mrs. Peabody wouldn't think of intruding, he and the girl followed the three riders up the trail for another hundred yards. At a sprawling ash tree growing along a pallid, oval alkali flat, they swung right off the trail and followed a deep-rutted two-track for another half a mile.

The trail crossed a semiwet creek murmuring softly over a bed of white stones, turned around a dilapidated corral, an unchinked log barn, and a chicken coop to pull up before a low-slung, tin-roofed cabin with a front porch missing as many floor planks as those still intact. Wan lamplight carried through the windows. Starlit sparkled on the tin roof, and the chimney pipe filled the air with the smell of roast beef and gravy.

"We've had a coupla tough years out here," said Jack

Gowdy, climbing heavily out of his saddle near the stopped carriage. "If it ain't coyotes, it's rustlers. If it ain't rustlers, it's drought or wildfires." He tossed his reins to the skinnier, younger boy, Kenny, and walked toward the buggy. "Beef'll be a mite stringy, but what we have is yours, Reverend. Let me give you a hand down."

The man took Longarm's arm, but as the lawman crawled out of the buggy and straightened to his full height, the man looked him up and down with a skeptical air. "Tall drink of water, ain't ya, Reverend? Forgive my surprise." He chuckled. "Where I come from, most men of the cloth are short, plump, and bald."

"No harm done, Brother Gowdy," Longarm said, turning to help Amber over the buggy's front wheel. "Say, how far would it be to Chugwater tomorrow? We'd like to stop there and have lunch with my lovely wife's aunt. . . ."

"You're almost there, Reverend. No more than a couple of hours. You'll make Chugwater by eleven o'clock and no later. I'd bet on it . . . if, of course, I was given to such devilish pursuits, which I certainly am not!"

Gowdy laughed with a brittle note of chagrin, then ordered his sons to put up the reverend's wagon. Leading Longarm and Amber up the porch steps, he apologized for the dilapidated condition of the environs and explained again about the rustlers, the drought, and the wildfires.

Inside the cabin, Gowdy's enormous wife, Muriel, was ecstatic to meet their devout guests. In fact, she and her tall, shapeless twin daughters, Agnes and Henrietta, literally fell all over themselves tidying up the place and adding a couple more plates to the long plank table that had already been set for six. The humble roast sat on the sideboard waiting for "Father," meaning Gowdy, to slice it.

Standing before him, broad as a barn door in her burlap sack dress, sweating, flushed, and looking about to faint, Mrs. Gowdy implored Longarm to say grace. She hadn't had a man of the cloth say grace at her table since her silly old Jack had wrenched her away from Minnesota what seemed like a lifetime ago. After confessing that she hadn't even

148

been to a church service in three years—the closest church was over to Chugwater and rumor had it the minister *imbibed*—she hoorawed her children and husband up to the table, sat herself down in a chair especially girded to support her two-hundred-plus pounds, closed her eyes, and bowed her head against her fists.

Amber glanced up nervously as Longarm stammered his way through a made-up prayer, compensating for his hesitation by showering the entire Gowdy family with blessings. Feeling bad about fooling the Gowdys—he was too far into the ruse to turn back now—and wishing like hell he could take a couple pulls of his Maryland rye, Longarm gave Amber a furtive wink and dug in.

The Gowdys, being typical country folk, didn't talk much over supper. That was fine with Longarm, who was fatigued not only from the long buggy ride but from the exertion of his preacher's guise. When supper was over, punctuated by dried apple pie, whipped cream, and coffee, there was a short-lived verbal tussle over who would sleep where. Muriel Gowdy wanted her husband and sons to sleep in the barn, turning the cabin's loft over to Longarm and Amber.

"Reverend and Mrs. Peabody" wouldn't hear of it, however. They were simple, God-fearin' folk who, when sleeping close to the earth and the animals, felt all the closer to God.

That decided, Longarm and Amber bid the Gowdys good night, and with an armload of bedding each, retired to an empty stable in a far corner of the barn. Longarm lit a rusty hurricane lantern, and they spread out their blankets side by side in the straw and began undressing.

As if reading each other's minds while casting tentative glances over their shoulders, neither stopped shucking off clothes until they stood facing each other as naked as the day they were born. Longarm chalked it up to shot nerves and piety fatigue when he ran his eyes up and down the girl's naked curves and said, "Stop me now if you aim to."

Amber's pale, pink-nippled breasts seemed to swell beneath his gaze. Her full lips parted as she dropped her eyes to his jutting member. A deep flush rose up from her neck. "I've never wanted anyone this bad, Custis."

"Good enough for me."

He stepped forward and engulfed her in his arms, clamping his mouth down on hers. When they'd kissed for a time, he eased her down into the hay and spread her legs. As she hooked her ankles behind his back, she thrust her hips up slightly. He thrust down, and then he was inside.

She groaned so loudly that he stopped, clamped his hand over her mouth, then slid deeper inside. He pulled halfway out, thrust in . . . out . . . in . . . until they were rocking together with such vigor, her heels pounding his back, that they'd soon tunneled into the straw mound behind them. When they'd finished, Longarm lifted his arm and shook himself like a dog, straw flying every which way.

Amber laughed, snaked her arms around his neck, rose up, and kissed him hard on the mouth. "I like you, Custis. I hope we don't die, but I reckon if I had to die with anyone, I'd just as soon it was with you."

"Thanks for the vote of confidence." He wrapped an arm beneath her and pulled her back out from beneath the straw mound. He lowered his hand and planted tender kisses on her rose-petal nipples, caressing creamy thigh with his hands. Brother Frye's black horse, stabled in the next stall, stared down at them with bemusement in his molasses-colored eyes.

Longarm nuzzled Amber's neck for a while, and ran his right hand through her silky snatch until he'd gotten her purring, teeth clattering with desire, then rolled her over. He kissed each of her dimpled, hay-flecked butt cheeks, then lifted her onto her knees. She lowered her head, reached down, grabbed his cock in her fist, and led him through her sopping portal, and he began pistoning in and out once more.

"You're soooo good," she said, her thin voice vibrating with each thrust. "You're really . . . really good . . . oh, *Gawd*!"

Ten minutes later, they slept.

Longarm felt as though he'd just closed his eyes when he

opened them again to see violet dawn light filtering through the windows . . . and his fully erect member half-buried in Amber's swollen mouth.

The Gowdy daughters, Agnes and Henrietta, had gotten up at four o'clock to bake bread while it was still cool.

They were kneading dough side by side at the long pine table in the kitchen when their mother lifted her head from the bed at the cabin's rear, beyond a four-by-four pole draped with coats, hats, and a lantern, and stared toward the girls. Her blue eyes were pale little marbles in the suety folds of her face, her long, silver-streaked hair tucked away behind her head like streamers of old corn silk.

"Girls, I just had a wonderful idea!"

Muriel Gowdy lifted her eyes to the ceiling, as if wishing she could share the idea with her husband, who slept upstairs with the boys. Because of the two-hundred-plus pounds she'd packed on since delivering Kendal, Muriel hadn't been able to climb the ladder for years. She and the girls slept together downstairs, which worked well since they had to be up before the others anyway.

"I wonder if Reverend Peabody would be so kind as to say a few words over Grandpa's grave."

Both girls looked up from their work. Their round, identical faces, owning their mother's pale-blue eyes and rosy cheeks, glistened with sweat. Strands of hair had fallen loose from the buns atop their heads.

"Do you think he would, Momma?" asked Agnes, slightly larger and rounder than her sister but otherwise identical.

"He never did have a *proper* burial," said Henrietta. "But . . . do you think it'd do any good now?"

"What on earth do you mean, child?"

"I mean," said Henrietta, as though it pained her to speak, "Pa said he mighta been turned down . . . the other way . . ."

"Don't say that!" Muriel scolded, rising up on her elbows to glare at the girl over the lumpy length of her quilt-mounded body. "Don't even think it. Your pa was just

151

foolin'. You know how he fools. Your grandfather is in heaven, singin' with the angels. Now, you run out to the barn—the Reverend's no doubt up and about by now, bein' a man of the cloth—and ask him if he'd be kind enough to say a few words over Grandpa's grave."

Henrietta hesitated, scowling down at the large lump of dough in which her fists were buried. Without lifting her head, she cut her timid eyes at her sister. "Will you come with me, Agnes?"

Agnes winced and looked at her mother. "Mama, I don't wanna talk to no preacher. Preachers make me nervous as all billy-heck!"

Her jowls shaking and her face flushing, Muriel Gowdy pushed herself up to a sitting position, and thrust her fat arm at the front door. "Get out there, both of you, and stop your fussin'!"

Five minutes later, Agnes and Henrietta left the cabin and stood side by side in the yard, glowering at the barn standing dark against the pale sky in which several stars still guttered.

"Don't see why the fat ole bitch can't ask the preacher her ownself," Agnes grumbled.

Henrietta knotted a scarf around her head, shivering in the early morning chill. "The old bastard's in hell anyway. Pa said so himself."

The girls started off across the yard, weaving around horse apples and cow pies.

"Best be quiet in case they're still asleep," Agnes said as she quietly pulled one of the barn's double doors open.

She slipped inside, and Henrietta followed, drawing the door closed behind her but leaving it unlatched. The barn was all shadows and misty edges. The smell of horse shit and piss wafted over the girls as they made their way down the narrow alley between the stalls, stepping over the drooping tongue of the hay wagon and the piles of tack the boys had been too lazy to hang up.

Henrietta stopped suddenly, grabbed her sister's arm.

"What?" Agnes whispered.

As if in reply, a deep grunt rose from the shadows at the

back of the barn. A woman moaned. The moan was sheathed in sucking sounds like those made by lambs drawing milk from a bottle.

Henrietta looked at Agnes, brows beetled. Agnes gave the same expression. As the girls stood staring at each other, listening to the moans, groans, sucking sounds, and occasional giggles rising from the back of the barn, Henrietta's lower jaw dropped.

"They're doin' the nasty!" she whispered.

Agnes covered her mouth with a pudgy hand, suppressing a laugh. "Come on," she said, her eyes bright with mischief. "Let's see if they do it the way Ma and Pa do it!"

The moans and groans and wet sounds got louder as the girls approached the barn's right rear stall. The black horse stared at them, a wary cast in its eyes. They stopped, afraid the horse was about to nicker. When the horse merely blinked and swung its head around to watch the activity in the next stall, Agnes crouched, tugging on her sister's arm. Both girls crawled on their hands and knees to the stall in question.

Agnes peeked through the slatted partition, and cupped her hand over her mouth to quash a startled exclamation.

"Jesus God!" the "preacher" exclaimed, releasing a long breath through gritted teeth.

There was a wet popping sound. The girl chuckled. "You like?"

"You ain't as innocent as you let on. . . ."

"Maybe not innocent, but I'm not—"

"Stay focused!"

When Henrietta pulled her head back from the narrow gap between the slats and looked at her sister, lower jaw hanging and eyes wide as fresh cow plop, Agnes tightened her stomach against a giggle. Clamping her hand against her mouth, she turned, beckoned to her sister, and scuttled silently away from the stall before scrambling to her feet and running, snorting into her hand, to the front of the barn and out the door.

Henrietta was close on her heels. When she had eased the

door shut, the girls dropped to their knees in paroxysms of restrained laughter. Henrietta caught her breath and looked up at Agnes with her hair in her eyes, her chubby red cheeks wet from tears.

"I ain't never seen *nothin'* like that!"

Agnes wiped tears from her own cheeks and smoothed a lock of hair from her eyes. "I'll tell you one thing—that ain't no preacher."

"Ain't no preacher's wife neither. You know who she is?"

Agnes gave her sister a knowing look. "Looks just like that showgirl those men who rode through here a couple days ago described. The one with the bounty on her head. You know what we could do that kind of money?"

"Are you thinkin' what I think you're thinkin'?"

"If you're thinkin' I'm thinkin' we should see if we can't scare us up a couple of prairie chickens around the Devil's Backbone, you're thinkin' right." Agnes held her finger to her lips. "Shhh. Don't let on."

She pounded the door with her fist and poked her head into the barn. "Reverend? Everybody decent in there . . . ?"

Chapter 18

It wasn't yet dawn before Longarm walked up the low knoll behind the Gowdys' cabin, flanked by Amber and the Gowdys themselves, and muttered what he remembered of the Lord's Prayer over Grandpa Gowdy's overgrown grave.

Feeling he had to add a few words of his own, he ended with, "Grant our brother in Heaven everlasting peace, Lord, and please give this fine family Peace on Earth until it's time, uh, for them to join you and Dear Old Grandpa in your blissful sanctuary up above the clouds."

He forgot and nearly crossed himself before muttering a simple Protestant "A-men," which the Gowdys echoed, Amber, whose mind had obviously wandered, following a full second later.

The prayer request had nearly caused him to spill the beans and tell the Gowdys who he really was, but what if bounty hunters came through here before Longarm could get Amber back to Chugwater?

Could the Gowdys keep a secret?

For Amber's sake, it was best to deceive them.

Shaking hands all around and accepting Mrs. Gowdy's sack of bacon and egg biscuits—Longarm didn't want to take time for breakfast—he and Amber set off on the last leg of their journey to Chugwater.

"Did you have fun this morning?" Amber asked when they were a mile out of the ranch yard, the jagged purple line of the Devil's Backbone rising slowly before them.

"You mean the . . . ? Of course I did. But don't worry, I don't think you're—"

"You seemed a little distracted there at the end."

Longarm bit off the end of his last cheroot. "That's cause we weren't alone."

Amber blinked up at him. "Huh?"

"We had us a coupla Peeping Toms. A couple of Peeping Henriettas and Agneses, I should say."

"Why didn't you say something? Why, those fat, little—!"

"I heard 'em scuttlin' around too late, and didn't see no reason to spoil their fun." Longarm chuckled and leaned forward to cup a lucifer to his cigar. "I could tell by the way they asked me to say a few words over their grandpap's grave that they'd figured out I wasn't a sky pilot, though. I just hope they haven't figured out *who we are* and spread it around. If there's anyone to spread it around to, that is."

Two hours later, the trail began climbing and winding around boulders toward the sandstone dike that resembled a dinosaur spine glistening like copper pennies in the mid-morning sun. Angling toward a gap between sandstone blocks at the crest of the ridge, Longarm suddenly turned the buggy off the left side of the trail.

Amber gave a startled exclamation. "What're you doing?"

Longarm stopped the buggy behind a boulder about two feet higher than the carriage, and set the brake. "This won't take but a minute." He grabbed his Winchester from under the seat, and rammed a shell into the chamber. "Stay here."

He leaped onto the boulder's flat top and dropped to his haunches. He snugged the Winchester butt to his shoulder and stared down the barrel. A sunbonnet-clad head poked out from behind a boulder about thirty yards downhill. The chubby body in a shapeless sack dress followed, crawling on all fours. In the girl's hand was an old Spencer saddle gun.

Longarm fired four quick rounds, blasting the ground and the rocks around Agnes's pudgy face.

His powder smoke wafting around him, he turned right. Forty yards behind, another sackcloth-draped figure—this one slightly smaller—bolted behind a cracked, triangular boulder. Longarm opened up until the echoes of six rifle shots chased themselves around the valley, fading slowly to be replaced by the whine of the ubiquitous Wyoming wind.

The side of the triangular boulder bore the chips and pocks of the .44-caliber slugs.

Two sets of wails rose simultaneously, and Longarm saw Henrietta sprint out from behind the boulder he'd just basted, while Agnes ran a twisting course through the rocks and sage on his left, on an interception course with her sister. Both girls were screaming as if their hair was on fire, waving their empty hands above their heads as though clawing at the air before them.

"Haul your fat asses home and stay there!" Longarm shouted through cupped hands, clamping his Winchester under his right arm.

When they were a hundred yards away, Henrietta tripped over a rock, fell, and rolled. Agnes kept heading for the broad-backed mule tied to a cottonwood another fifty yards beyond, her ass shifting in her dress like forty pounds of pudding.

Henrietta climbed heavily to her feet and stuck her right middle finger up at Longarm. "Fuck you, Mr. Donkey-dong!"

Longarm triggered another shot from the hip. The slug blew up a bunchgrass clump three feet in front of Henrietta's right foot. She leaped straight back, nearly falling. Her terrified yelp reached Longarm as she wheeled and took off after her sister, gaining the mule.

Longarm turned, leaped from the rock into the buggy, and shoved his rifle under the seat. "Bitches."

"I hope you salted 'em good, Custis."

"They've seen the error of their ways." Longarm turned the black back onto the trail, angling for the gap in the Devil's Backbone. "Let's just hope that's the last setback we see today."

• • •

Sitting under the brush arbor before the stone jailhouse in Chugwater; his boots crossed on a three-legged footstool, Jim Friendly removed the loosely wrapped quirley from his lips and, blowing smoke out his nose, stared thoughtfully at the gray coal.

It was mid-morning. Longarm hadn't appeared yet. Would he, or would Friendly have to turn the dwarf back loose on the town?

In spite of his frayed nerves, the sheriff yawned. He hadn't been sleeping well. In fact, he'd probably gotten only about a single hour's worth of good shut-eye in the past nine.

He was about to return the quirley to his mouth when the door clicked behind his right shoulder. He jumped with a start, and turned to see one of his four deputies, Lon Kitchen, step through the open doorway holding a covered slop bucket by its wire handle. Lon wore a distasteful expression on his coyotelike, mustachioed face.

He closed the door behind him and curled his upper lip. "Little bastard sure does piss and shit a lot. And, pee-ewe, does it stink! I don't mind tellin' you, Sheriff, I'm gettin' right tired of emptying his thunder mugs."

"His lawyer still in there?"

"Yeah."

"Should've had *him* do it." Friendly indulged in a grin as he drew a deep drag on the cigarette. As the deputy walked past him with the slop bucket, heading for the privy out back, he said, "Next time, give it to the albino to empty. Tell him it's my orders."

Kitchen chuckled as he disappeared around the jailhouse's right front corner, the mid-morning sun glinting on his oiled, black hair. "You got it, Sheriff."

Friendly had just put his boots back up on the footstool when a voice sounded from above. "Sheriff Friendly!"

Friendly stood and walked out into the street before the jailhouse, turning to peer up at the jailhouse roof. His youngest deputy, the red-headed, suspender-clad Jeff Crowley, sat on the shake-roofed peak, staring southwest through his field glasses, the lenses glinting in the intensifying light. He stared at the deputy expectantly. He'd hoped the young deputy was hailing the arrival of Longarm and the girl.

"Light rig headed this way. Just now crossin' Little Goose Creek. A two-seater with four passengers." The deputy lowered the binoculars and glanced down at his boss. "Looks like the judge and Mr. Hallam, Sheriff."

Friendly cursed. He'd hoped Longarm and the girl would have arrived before the circuit judge and county attorney, both of whom, their private secretaries in tow, never liked to let grass grow under their feet in this sunbaked little backwater.

"Anything in the north?"

The red-haired, freckled-faced deputy turned up the street and lifted the glasses to his eyes, the lenses shaded by the brim of his black slouch hat. He shook his head. "Nope. Sorry, Sheriff. I'll yell soon as I spy 'em."

Friendly turned southwestward again, sucking the quirley and shading his eyes with his left hand. Just now the horse and carriage appeared, little more than a shadow from this distance, climbing the rise up from the creek, pushing a slice of purple shade along before it.

"I'll be inside," Friendly growled.

He pushed through the office door, glanced at Deputy Wes MacGregor oiling a rifle on the bench along the left wall, and looked into the dwarf's cell at the back of the room. The dwarf and the dwarf's albino lawyer were playing poker. Such activity wasn't allowed—only official consultations, one hour per day—but Friendly overlooked it. Let the lawyer keep his client entertained, so the dwarf wasn't whining and complaining about his pillow, his chamber pot, or constantly demanding food, coffee, or tobacco. Friendly had almost shot the little man once, and he was liable to try it again.

Doing so, he very well knew, would enrage the dwarf's hired gunmen, and ignite a powder keg.

A wet stogie wedged in his mouth, the dwarf turned to the sheriff. "Hey, Friendly, any sign of that federal badge-toter and the girl?" He sneered.

"Nope." Friendly poured a cup of coffee at the stove. "But the judge and prosecutor are workin' their way up from the creek. Won't be long, now"—Friendly cast a smile over his right shoulder—"before we're buildin' a gallows."

The dwarf chuckled. "Only if the girl makes it, Sheriff. Only if the girl makes it. Goddamnit, Mort—call or raise, will ya?"

A few minutes later, a shadow passed over the curtained window. Friendly took a sip of coffee, drowned his cigarette in the mug, straightened his hat, and tried smoothing the wrinkles from his blue wool shirt and vest.

Voices rose outside, and he stood as the office door opened. The judge's dapper personal secretary, with his derby hat, tiny round spectacles, and full red beard, entered the office. He was followed by Judge Olaf Blackwood himself, standing straight as a cedar post in his black suit and polished half-boots, his gold watch chain glinting and gray muttonchops framing his brick-red cheeks like wide strips of lamb's wool. The judge had a nose like a doorstop, the blue veins splattered from drink.

"Hello, Jim," said the jurist, doffing his black derby as two other men followed him into the jailhouse. He glanced into the rear cell as he inquired of Friendly, "How the hell you been?"

Friendly stood and hooked his thumbs behind his cartridge belt. Deputy MacGregor gained his feet and set the rifle on the bench, flushing slightly and cutting his nervous eyes at Friendly. It was always a little nerve-racking, having the phlegmatic old jurist in town, though he came only when needed. Out here there wasn't the customary separation between the judiciary and law enforcement, and the judge tended to play the role of an Army major visiting his rowdy far-flung troops.

"Can't complain," said Friendly.

"How's Mary Lou?"

"Owly as ever."

The judge chuckled and glanced at the deputy. "How're you, McCarthy?"

MacGregor corrected the judge with a shy grin and told him he was fit as a fiddle. No, it wasn't his wife who was expecting the baby—in fact, he wasn't even married. Deputy Kitchen's wife was the one in the family way.

Meanwhile, the county prosecutor, Burt Hallam—a slightly younger version of the judge—brushed copper-colored dust from his claw-hammer coat, smoothed his waxed mustache with his fingers, and joined in the pre-business banter. Both men's personal secretaries flanked them near the door, looking bored and uncomfortable in their dust-caked suits and hats, as well as sunburned and sweaty. It had been a long ride from Laramie.

Finally, the prosecutor, Hallam, turned toward the cell at the back of the room, where both the dwarf and the dwarf's albino attorney stood at the door, the albino ridiculously taller than his client. They could have been a pair of freaks in any carnival sideshow, and Friendly repressed the urge to snicker.

"So, let's get down to business," Hallam said with a bemused air, smoothing his mustache as he scrutinized the pair.

Before Friendly could speak, the albino asked to be let out of the cell. When Friendly had released the defense attorney, the men gathered around Friendly's desk, upon which the sheriff spread the telegrams he'd exchanged with Miss Amber Rogers, and recounted his reasons, as objectively as possible, why he was holding the dwarf on the charge of murder in the first degree. The dwarf interrupted several times from his cell, but the albino successfully waved him silent. Apparently, he'd counseled the dwarf on his conduct in front of the judge.

"You do know, of course, Your Honor, that telegrams are hardly conclusive evidence," J. Mortimer St. Paul said when Friendly had spoken his piece to the judge and prosecutor. "A telegram can be sent by anyone . . . *signed* by anyone. There is no proof these missives were sent by Miss Rogers or by anyone who knows . . ."

"Don't read us the law, Mr. St. Paul," said Hallam. "I'll

prosecute when I see enough evidence, and it'll my decision, not *yours*."

On it went until the judge told Friendly, as he and the prosecutor had both mentioned in letters and telegrams, that the case boiled down to the girl's word against the dwarf's. A jury would have to decide whom to believe. But if the girl wasn't in town by noon, Friendly would have to release the dwarf, and the judge and prosecuting attorney would be on their way to the next town on their itinerary.

When Friendly looked at Hallam for help, the prosecutor shook his head. "You know the law of this territory as well as I do, Jim. You can hold a prisoner until the circuit judge arrives to try him, but you have to try him promptly or set him free. Since the girl has not yet appeared, and since you've already been holding Mr. Turley for seven days, we'll give her and the federal lawman till noon. As I told you in my letter, I'm not optimistic. Who's a jury going to believe—a respected businessman or a showgirl?"

"Businessman?" Friendly shouted. "Christ, he's a hoodlum. He has all of this town's legitimate businessmen in a stranglehold!"

"Prove it," the dwarf said from his cell, his thick, beringed fingers clutching the bars. He stared up with his nostrils flared and upper lip curled.

The albino glanced at him, then turned back to Friendly, rising up and down on the balls of his patent leather shoes.

With that, Hallam and the judge donned their hats and turned to their secretaries holding satchels by the door. "I need food and drink," said the judge as his secretary held out his hat.

"Try the Dwarf House," the dwarf said with a chuckle. "Best hooch and vittles—not to mention girls—in the territory. I'll be showin' Cheyenne how to dance in a year or two!"

As the four suited gents left the jailhouse, Friendly followed them out. He closed the door behind him as the men mounted their dusty black carriage, which squawked and

162

clattered beneath their weight, the clean-lined bay rippling its withers and snorting.

"Try Old Miguel's Café beside the livery barn," Friendly said. "He's got the best tripe in the county, and you won't have to worry about your money goin' to support that little privy rat's extortion and murder."

" 'Preciate the advice, Jim," the judge said as his secretary released the brake and shook the reins over the bay's back. "Track us down when the girl shows up, will you?"

Friendly watched the buggy jounce off down the street, heading for the livery barn at the far end of town.

"If she shows up."

Friendly turned. The albino stood behind him, umbrella open, black-gloved right hand raising a long, thin cigar to his lips, the pink-lidded rabbit eyes narrowed with a sneer.

"She'll show up, asshole. I sent the best federal lawman in the territory after her." Feigning a casual air, Friendly sat in the chair in which he'd been sitting before, tipped it back, crossed his boots on the footstool, and entwined his hands behind his head. "She'll show up."

"Yes, well, if . . . I mean *when* she does, send a deputy for me, will you?" the albino said. "I'll be at the Dwarf House."

Friendly watched the albino tramp prissily up street, waiting for a ranch wagon to pass, then doing a little hop-skip as he made his way toward the Dwarf House, standing like a great red hemorrhoid on the lip of the asshole that Chugwater had become since the dwarf's arrival.

Friendly was rolling another quirley and staring north between the business district's false facades when his fingers quit working. At the end of town, Judge Blackwood, Prosecutor Hallam, and their two secretaries stood on the boardwalk before the Dwarf House, conversing as they looked up at the massive, red-painted structure before them.

"Don't do it, assholes," Friendly growled, staring, his hands frozen on the rolling paper to which he'd applied a thin line of tobacco.

Finally, the judge turned to Hallam. Both men inspected

the steep steps rising to the Dwarf House's broad front porch on which several girls in bright, skimpy dresses lounged, smoking and taking some sun. Hallam shrugged, turned to say something to the secretaries, who nodded, then stepped abreast of the judge. Both men climbed the stairs, their assistants following two steps directly behind.

Two of the pleasure girls leaned over the railing, smiling down at the four suits climbing toward them, their lips moving, but Friendly was too far away to hear what they said. The judge smiled in return and ticked his hat brim. Hallam waved.

"Bastards," Friendly said.

Chapter 19

After an hour of hard climbing, Longarm and Amber finally surmounted the often-treacherous crest of the Devil's Backbone. The rocks of the spine were so closely spaced in places that Longarm had to get out and shift the buggy's back end around by hand.

On the opposite slope, it was smooth trailing for a mile. Then they reached a wash choked with boulders and driftwood and large dirt clumps from the previous spring's flood. There was no way through the debris, so Longarm turned the buggy first west along the wash, then east before he finally found a ford.

The manuever cost him and Amber nearly an hour, and by the time they crested a rise from which they could see the little burg of Chugwater nestled in steep chalky buttes and abutted in the south by a broad, dry river, it was nearly noon.

And they still had about a thousand yards to go. . . .

Longarm continued on down the rise, hoorawing the tired black into a gallop. They'd nearly leveled out when Amber sucked a sharp breath and said, "There!"

Longarm looked at her, then followed her gaze off the trail to his left. About a hundred yards away, two riders galloped toward them, spaced about twenty yards apart. They crested a chalky hogback, then disappeared into a crease on

Longarm's side of the rise, only their pallid dust visible, the muffled clatter of their horses' hooves rising faintly above the breeze and the raucous scolding of prairie dogs on the trail's right side.

"Take it easy," Longarm said, slowing the black to a trot. "Keep your veil over your eyes and your head down."

"They have to be the dwarf's rannies," Amber said, her voice quivering slightly. "What if they recognize me?"

"All those boys are gonna see is my preacher's collar. Mark my words, they'll wave us on."

"What about him?"

Longarm glanced at her. She was staring off across the prairie dog town. Another rider moved toward them across a flat, his black duster and string tie blowing out behind him. He held his derby on his head with one hand. The wind revealed the two iron-filled shoulder holsters under the duster, in addition to another hogleg positioned for the cross-raw on his left hip.

Longarm cursed silently. He dug a tobacco fleck between his two front teeth with his tongue, adjusted the preacher's collar, and tried to sound optimistic. "Him too. Ease back into your seat. Look relaxed and, since you're a preacher's wife, look friendly too."

She forced a smile as she said through gritted teeth, "Look friendly at someone who is looking to kill me and toss me in a ravine. Anything else?"

"That should do it for now."

Thuds rose on both sides of the trail. The black whinnied and the horse of the rider on the right side of the trail replied in kind. That rider was the first to reach the trail about twenty yards ahead of the buggy, and he checked his claybank down, resting one hand on the grips of his cross-draw .45.

The other two rode up across from him. The three swung their horses toward Longarm and Amber, blocking the trail. The man on the far left reached down to shuck a Winchester from his saddle boot, cock it one-handed, then rest the barrel across his saddle bows as he stared toward the approaching buggy, slitting his eyes against the sun.

He was a big man in a suit that looked too small. Long, blond hair fell down from his dusty, black slouch hat.

Longarm kept his smile in place as he sawed back on the black's reins. "Good afternoon, brothers."

The blond gent signaled the other two riders with a glance. As they gigged their horses forward, circling the wagon like vultures while eyeing Longarm and the girl suspiciously, the blond gent remained where he was, staring through one eye, head cocked suspiciously. When the other two had circled the buggy once, they spurred their mounts back up to the blond gent, neck-reining their horses in tight circles to sit staring back at Longarm and Amber like hawks awaiting fresh kill.

The blond gent rolled a matchstick from one side of his mouth to the other. "Where you headed, Reverend?" He curled his lip as he slid his gaze to Amber. "Ma'am."

Amber said nothing as Longarm replied, "Cheyenne by way of Chugwater. If we're trespassin' on private property, we apologize."

The blond gent rolled the matchstick back to the other side of his mouth. "You ain't trespassin'. We're just, uh, keepin' tabs on the trail to Chugwater, that's all. We wouldn't want any bad element comin' in and, you know, causin' trouble."

The other two men smiled at that while keeping their eyes on Longarm and the girl.

Longarm smiled. "Well, I assure you, my wife and I are the very enemy of trouble. Now, if you'd be so kind, we'll be on our way. . . ."

The blond gent nibbled the match, then glanced at the two men beside him. All three shifted their gazes between Longarm and Amber. As the buggy pulled directly between the men, the blond gent aimed the rifle straight out from his right hip, the barrel pointed between Longarm and Amber.

"Hold up there."

Longarm pulled back on the ribbons. His heart quickened. He stared at the blond gent, feeling his smile go cold.

"Ma'am," the blond gent said, gesturing with the Winchester barrel, "would you mind lifting that veil so's I can see your face?"

Longarm felt Amber tense beside him, saw her glance at him in the corner of his right eye. Canting his head to one side, the blond gent stretched his lips back from his teeth clamped down on the lucifer, and wagged the rifle at her. His voice hardened. "Lift it."

Longarm heard Amber swallow. He grinned. "Go ahead, my heart. The man just wants to see your lovely face."

Amber's cheeks bleached behind the veil, and her lids were drawn back so far that Longarm thought her eyes would pop from their sockets. Turning toward the blond gent, Amber reached up and began lifting the vale with her right hand. When she'd lifted the veil as far as her forehead, Longarm snaked his right hand across his waist, filled his fist with his Colt .44-40.

The blond gent snapped his eyes back to Longarm, gritting his teeth as Longarm clicked back the hammer. As the blond gent shifted the rifle toward him, Longarm's Colt barked and smoked.

A thimble-sized hole appeared in the man's left temple, just beneath his hat brim. The horse pitched and whinnied at the shot, throwing the blond gent straight back over the horse's rump. Longarm swung the Colt right.

"Hey!" the man on the left screamed as he palmed his own revolver.

He didn't get the gun raised higher than his belly before Longarm's slug plowed through the left center of his chest.

Pow!

Longarm's Colt spoke again, but the other rider's horse pitched, and the bullet merely blew the brown derby from the man's head. Jerking back on his horse's reins, the rider leveled his long-barreled Remington and fired. As the slug tore the air left of Longarm's head, the lawman fired again. The rider winced and grabbed his upper right shoulder, his horse pitching him off the trail.

The black pitched too, and lunged forward, the buggy rocking ahead with several nasty jolts. Amber screamed and grabbed the seat as the black whinnied and, shaking its head, began pounding hooves and lifting dust toward Chugwater.

Longarm picked up the reins and was about to holster the .44 when a pistol barked behind him. Amber ducked, holding her hat on her head. Longarm peered back over his right shoulder.

The surviving member of the three riders was galloping after them, hatless, leaning forward and triggering shots with the pistol in his extended right hand.

"Keep your head down," Longarm ordered the girl, then turned and aimed the Colt behind the leaping, clattering buggy. He triggered two shots, but the buggy was jolting too hard for accurate shooting, and the rider gained ground steadily, gritting his teeth and slinging lead, his black hair winging out behind him.

Longarm pulled the trigger once more, but the hammer clicked, empty. He cursed, holstered the weapon, and yelled above the thudding hooves and clattering wheels, "Can you keep this thing on the trail?"

"I'll try!" Amber leaned forward and reached for the reins, the wind whipping the hat from her head.

When she had control of the flying black, and while bullets buzzed around them from behind, Longarm reached down for the Winchester and levered a round into the chamber.

Sitting in front of the jailhouse, boots crossed on the three-legged stool before him, Jim Friendly plucked his old silver turnip watch from his vest pocket, and flipped the lid. Twelve-twenty-three.

"Goddamnit."

He looked over the open lid and down the sunlit tunnel of the main drag to the thin ribbon of trail twisting through the bald buttes beyond, bright as bleached flower in the unforgiving noon. The sun was straight up, and the shadows of the businesses along Main were snugged up tight against the boardwalks.

Not many people on the street this time of day, everyone inside the Dwarf House or the Chinaman's place or the Mexican's, eating dinner. A big ranch dray was parked before the mercantile about halfway down and on the right side of the street, two of Owen Lang's hired men wrestling fence posts and rolls of Glidden wire from the raised loading dock and onto the wagon's bed.

Aside from the desultory chatter of the ranch men, and the thumps of the supplies hitting the wagon bed, there wasn't a sound.

"Goddamnit!" Friendly said again, lifting his gaze once more to the buttes beyond the town, where nothing stirred. No mare's tails of dust licked up behind those buttes, signaling oncoming riders.

Up the street on the left, door hinges squawked, and voices rose. Three men appeared on the Dwarf House's raised porch—the county prosecutor, the albino, and the prosecutor's little, suited secretary, the man's spectacles glinting yellow in the harsh light. The trio stepped over to the porch's outer rail, stared across the street at Friendly. They spoke amongst themselves, then turned and began descending the long steps toward the street.

Friendly snapped the watch lid closed. Something heavy sank within him, settled deep. He'd sent a good man into a gauntlet, gotten him and an innocent girl killed. And nothing in Chugwater had changed. It was still headed to the perdition to which it had been headed before Friendly had received the girl's first telegram.

He stood stiffly as Hallam, the albino, and the secretary angled toward him, their shoes kicking up dust puffs as they stepped around manure piles in the wide street. The albino was smiling, half-sneering, his pale hair hanging loosely down around his pallid face, rabbit eyes slitted beneath the umbrella he held above his head.

Behind them, three of the dwarf's hired derby-hatted thugs stepped onto the Dwarf House's broad porch, two holding rifles while another wore a brace of pistols in shoulder holsters.

Friendly lifted his chin and said, "Anything on the horizon, Jeff?"

After a moment, the deputy on the jailhouse roof said

fatefully, "Nothin', Sheriff. Not a damn thing . . ."

The three suited men approached on the street before him. Hallam opened his mouth to speak, but Friendly held up his right hand, palm out. "Wait here."

As the three stopped in front of the stoop, Friendly turned and pushed through the jail office door. Deputies Lon Kitchen and Wes MacGregor stood at the window to Friendly's right. They'd been peering out, but now they turned to Friendly with dejected expressions on their hollow, unshaven faces.

"Shit," MacGregor said knowingly.

Leaving the door open behind him, Friendly crossed to his desk. He grabbed the keys from the second drawer on the right, then continued to the back of the office. The dwarf stood facing him, hands clutching the bars of his cell door. The corners of his mouth turned up, and his leathery cheeks dimpled. He chuckled.

"Don't take it so hard, Jim."

Friendly glowered down at the little, bullet-headed gent who'd already donned his frock coat and derby hat and tucked his shirttails into his broadcloth trousers. When Friendly opened the door, the dwarf ambled out, swaying from side to side on his bowed legs, his child-sized boots snick-snicking across the earthen floor.

The little man stopped and ran his thumb and index finger along his hat brim. "Look at it this way. The town's gonna do nothin' but grow."

"Yeah, it'll grow, all right," Lon Kitchen said as he stood on the other side of Friendly's desk, squeezing his Springfield carbine in his hands as he scowled down at the dwarf. "But in what way? How many more good folks are you gonna make disappear when they can't pay your tax?"

MacGregor gritted his teeth and balled his fists as he moved toward the dwarf. "Let me take care of this little—"

Friendly clamped his hand on the deputy's shoulder. "Wes!"

MacGregor stopped, continued staring at the dwarf, breathing loudly through his nose.

The dwarf laughed and sauntered toward the open door and the three men waiting in the street beyond. "Lon, Wes, it's been a pleasure." At the door, he stopped and looked at Friendly over his left shoulder. "You too, Jim. We'll, uh"—he glanced from Friendly to the deputies and back again, his eyes narrowing with menace—"see ya around."

With that he turned, moved through the door, and clapped his hands together once as he walked out into the street. "Ah, *sweet freedom*!"

Chapter 20

As the dwarf started back to his rambling red saloon with the albino, Hallam, and Hallam's secretary, Sheriff Friendly kicked the door shut with such fury that the entire room shook and dust sifted down from the rafters.

Friendly turned and tossed the keys in the open drawer. While the deputies stood on the other side of his desk in moody silence, the sheriff grabbed his hat off the rack behind his chair, and put it on.

"I'm headin' home, fellas. Wes, why don't you go on home and get some sleep. Lon, mind the shop till—"

Friendly stopped as the snaps of gunfire rose faintly amidst the noontime quiet. The other two deputies, whose hearing was keener than the sheriff's, were already half turned toward the door with their heads cocked.

"What the hell's that?" Friendly said as he moved to the door, opened it, and stepped onto the boardwalk, peering up the street. He lifted his chin a little, and raised his voice. "Jeff, where's the shootin' comin' from?"

"Damn," said the deputy atop the jailhouse. "A buggy's comin' in like a damn cyclone. Horse and rider about twenty yards behind. They're *shootin'* at each other!"

Friendly stared up the trail snaking north through the chalky, sage-tufted buttes. A black speck angled out from behind a bullet-shaped butte from the crest of which a lone pine jutted. The black speck followed the long curve for fifty feet before a lone rider appeared behind the pine-topped butte, smoke puffs rising from just above the horse's head and above the jostling buggy, the pistol and rifle reports following a second behind each puff.

Friendly's heartbeat quickened. He glanced left.

The dwarf and the three other men were stopped just this side of the Dwarf House, staring up the street. Hallam had stepped off the boardwalk and raised his hand to shade his eyes.

The dwarf's voice rose sharply. "What the fuck's that about?"

Friendly walked into the center of the street, his two deputies flanking him, his hand resting on his pistol grips. He poked his hat brim back as the buggy grew larger at the far end of town, until the black horse separated from the black splotch of the buggy and the two people on the single, leather seat—a tall, black-clad gent and a woman in a dark dress and wearing a dark box hat. The woman was steering the buggy while the black-clad gent twisted around in his seat, firing a rifle behind them.

Longarm, Friendly thought, his stomach turning eager somersaults. It had to be!

The wagon gained the far end of town and came on toward the jailhouse, seventy yards and closing, the black's hooves thudding and the buggy wheels clattering.

Friendly unholstered his Remington and began jogging up the street, shouting over his right shoulder at the two deputies, "It's Longarm and the witness!"

At the same time, Longarm drew a bead on the trailing rider's chest.

"Rein him in!" Longarm yelled to Amber.

As the girl yelled "Whoooah!" and sawed back on the black's reins, Longarm squinted his left eye, held his breath, and squeezed the Winchester's trigger. The man's head and shoulders jerked back, and his pistol flew out of his hand.

His claybank buck-kicked suddenly as it caught up to the slowing buggy, and swerved hard to the right. The shooter tumbled off the right side of the saddle and, as the horse headed for an alley mouth along the north side of the street, the man's body careened toward Longarm.

"Look out!" the lawman shouted, leaning toward the left front wheel while Amber ducked and leaned right.

The shooter's body hit the back of the seat and slid, belly up, until the man's head rested against the floorboard between Longarm's and the girl's feet, blood pumping from the hole in his chest, his eyes glazed with death, mouth forming a grimace. His boots were hung up on the back of the seat, and his eyes hung slack, jerking slightly with the death spasms.

As the buggy rocked to a halt, Amber regarded the man with disgust. Longarm raked his gaze from the dead shooter to three men jogging toward them—Jim Friendly and two deputies.

Friendly had his hogleg drawn. His eyes locked with Longarm's, and the sheriff stopped suddenly, a grin tugging at his mouth corners until he turned to see the Dwarf House rising along the street to his right.

The broad front porch boasted five or six brawny, well-dressed men in shirtsleeves, four-in-hand ties, and derby hats . . . wielding pistols or rifles. As they stared cow-eyed over the railing at the buggy, Longarm slid his gaze to another small group gathered on the street below, near the mouth of the stairs.

Three men, one of whom was an albino holding a tan umbrella, and a child. No, not a child. That was the dwarf standing there staring back at Longarm, gritting his small, square teeth and puffing his cheeks in and out.

Stretched seconds passed. Silence except for the blowing, nickering black and an incredulous murmur rising from the scantily clad women on the balcony behind the dwarf's armed toughs.

Longarm, Amber, Friendly, and the sheriff's deputies cut their gazes between the balcony of armed toughs and the little group at the bottom of the stairs. The dwarf and his men stared back.

Friendly turned toward the dwarf and his lawyer and said tightly, "Dwarf, get your ass back in the jailhouse."

Longarm's heart beat erratically. His Winchester was nearly empty, as he'd emptied it at the shooter trailing them out of the buttes. His Colt too was filled with only empty cartridges.

"Fuck you, Sheriff!" The dwarf stepped suddenly out from the shade cast by the albino's umbrella, and raised his short arm, jerking his beringed right finger at the buggy. "Shoot that fucking bitch! Shoot her!"

Longarm said, "Hold on," as he grabbed the reins from Amber and jerked them across the black's sweat-silvered back.

"Gidyup, horse!" he shouted as gunfire erupted on the balcony. "Haul your mangy assss!"

The horse lurched forward with a shrill whinny. As bullets began plunking into the buggy's leather seat and barking off the iron-shod wheels and hammering the wooden frame, Longarm jerked Amber down to the floor atop the dead man.

At the same time, the lawman swung the horse into the nearest alley mouth to his left, shouting at the top of his lungs and wincing at the bullets buzzing around his ears and snapping the buggy's roof stays and guide straps. He was halfway down the alley when one bullet grazed the left side of his head, just above his ear, and another blew nap from the shoulder of his black frock.

Amber yowled. Longarm looked down to see her wincing while holding her left hand over her left arm, blood oozing from just above her elbow.

"Hold on!" he yelled as, at the end of the alley, he jerked the black hard right. The buggy was only halfway through the turn before the right wheel clipped a rain barrel.

Amber screamed as the right side of the buggy bounced into the air. Longarm grabbed her arm and kicked off the buggy floor. He hit the alley on his left shoulder, bringing the girl down on top of him. Their momentum flung them

it into the back lot between a privy and a chicken coop, the
rl groaning as they rolled over and under each other, Long-
m finally coming to rest on his back and looking up
rough a cloud of dust.

Amber lay sprawled across his chest, her hair in his face.
he din of angry gunfire rose from Main Street—so many
ns that it sounded like a small war playing out. Friendly
d his deputies were trying to hold off the dwarf's toughs.

A horse whinnied, and Longarm turned to see the black
agging the buggy eastward down the alley behind the
ain Street shops, the buggy bouncing and kicking up dust
d the horse lunging and shaking its head. The left wheel
oke off and rolled up against a firewood pile.

Longarm looked at Amber. "You all right?"

She sat up, holding her arm. "Had a soft landing, but my
m hurts like hell! It's just a burn, though."

"You still willin' to testify against that little bastard?"

She whipped her head up, throwing her dusty hair back
om her eyes, and gritted her teeth. "You bet your ass!"

Longarm smiled and grabbed her good arm. "Let's go!"

Longarm picked his Winchester up out of the dust and
urried along the alley in the same direction the black had
one, thumbing cartridges into his Winchester's loading
ate. Amber tagged along behind him, holding her skirts
ove her ankles with one hand, clamping her wounded arm
her side like a broken wing. The gunfire on the other side
the shops on their rights grew louder and heavier.

"What the hell's goin' on up there, mister?"

Longarm turned to see an old man with a scraggly beard,
eeve garters, and a green eyeshade hunkered down behind
woodpile on his left. An old lady cowered beside him, her
ad in her arms. The old man peered up above the wood-
le, scowling at Longarm.

"They done blew out all the glass in my jewelry shop!"

Longarm kept moving, kicking a tin can. "Just stay down,
d-timer. War's bein' waged, but it'll be over soon if I have
ything to say about it!"

When they'd jogged to the other end of Main, weaving

177

around cribs, privies, woodpiles, and trash heaps, Longarm and Amber stopped at the east rear corner of the mud-and brick harness shop. Twenty yards away lay the stone jail house. The Dwarf House was back in the other direction and all the shooting was coming from there.

The alley and the jailhouse appeared to be clear.

Longarm took Amber's hand and, holding the rifle in his other hand, said, "Come on!"

He slanted across the twenty-yard gap and pressed his left shoulder against the jailhouse, squeezing Amber's hand as he hurried up along the jailhouse's north wall to the front corner. Turning the corner, then pausing to swing Amber ahead of him, he glanced to his right.

A block away, the giant, red Dwarf House stood gauzed in gunsmoke. Pistols and rifles flashed and roared along both sides of the street. A body lay in the dirt beneath the balcony, a rifle crossed on the dead man's ankles.

Longarm turned and shoved Amber through the jail house's open door. Amber screamed as a man wheeled from Friendly's cluttered desk, ramming home the cocking lever of the rifle in his hands and aiming the rifle straight out from his shoulder.

Her shoulder.

Mary Lou's auburn hair flew about her red cheeks and angry-bright eyes, and she gritted her teeth savagely.

Longarm shoved Amber aside and stepped forward. "Hold on, Mary Lou—it's Custis Long!"

Mary Lou lowered the rifle, surprise shouldering aside the anger in her eyes. She shuttled her gaze between Longarm and Amber. "Cuttin' it kind of close, aren't ya?"

"What're you doin'?"

Mary Lou plucked a shell from the open box on her father's desk, and slid it through the Winchester's loading gate. "Headin' out to help Pa."

Longarm shook his head. "I'll help your pa. You stay here with Amber." He moved to the door and swung back around. The girls stared at him, incredulous and scared, Amber lutching her right forearm. "Any of the dwarf's boys head his way, give 'em a pill they can't digest!"

"I ain't gonna ask 'em to dance!" Mary Lou yelled as he wung around and headed back the way he and Amber had come.

He ran back to where the old couple were cowering behind the woodpile, then threaded a gap between store buildings to Main Street, the mouth of the gap putting him nearly directly in front of the Dwarf House. Nearby pistol shots ounded on his right and, crouching behind a rain barrel on he boardwalk before Tate's Jewelry, Longarm turned to see im Friendly lying behind a stock trough, snaking his revolver around the end close to Longarm, and triggering a hot toward the Dwarf House balcony.

"Jim, it's Custis!" Longarm shouted. There seemed to be bout five men slinging lead from the Dwarf House, two uddled behind barrels on the porch. They kept up a deafening din.

Friendly snapped a look at him, snarling, his hat off and lood from a bullet burn trickling down his right temple. What'd you do—stop for tea?"

Longarm ducked as a bullet fired from the balcony barked nto the rain barrel, flinging slivers. "Somethin' like that." He lanced around, spotting one of Friendly's deputies to his left, oled up behind the right rear wheel of a green farm wagon. Another was on the same side of the street as the Dwarf House, shooting from behind a woodpile to its left Longarm aw close rifle shots beyond Friendly, where smoke puffs indicated a man positioned on the far side of the harness shop.

Longarm aimed his Winchester at the balcony, and fired. A man yowled as the .44 slug spanged off a rifle stock, and he derby-hatted head on the right side of the porch suddenly ucked behind a barrel. Longarm ejected the spent shell and lanced at Friendly, who was reloading his six-shooter.

"Jim, I'm gonna circle around, enter the pipsqueak's lair rom the back. Give me five minutes, then you and your boys eally raise some hell!"

179

"Careful who you shoot in there, Custis!" Friendly sai
He snapped his Remington's loading gate closed and spu
the cylinder. He looked up at Longarm, and sneered. "Th
judge and prosecuting attorney are in there!"

"'Preciate the warning!" Longarm shouted, then ducke
as two more rifle shots hammered his rain barrel. He bolte
off his heels and ran back through the gap between the build
ings. A couple of slugs tore up dirt at his boots before h
flew around the corner of the building on his left, an
sprinted back toward the other end of town.

Three minutes later, he was on the other side of the mai
drag, tramping down the alley toward the rear of the Dwar
House, hearing the muffled gunfire ahead and left. Holdin
the Winchester straight up and down, he wove through sev
eral piles of tarp-covered firewood and around a stinkin
privy. He mounted a broad loading dock, and pressed hi
back up against the saloon–brothel's rear wall, left of tw
massive wooden doors—the old freight entrance, no doubt.

He waited, listening.

The gunfire increased, a staccato racket that made th
boards behind Longarm's back bounce.

"Thanks, Jim."

He grabbed a door handle, pulled, lowered the Winches
ter's barrel, and bolted into the musty shadows.

Chapter 21

Longarm left the door open behind him and stepped to one side, jerking his head around.

He was in a large storeroom with a high ceiling and a loft lit only by the light emanating from the open door and the knots in the whipsawed pine boards. The room still smelled of milled flour from the building's previous life, but now it seemed to house only whiskey and beer barrels, which added their own distinctive aromas.

The gunfire caused dust to sift from the rafters and the chimney of an unlit lantern to ring like a bell. Somewhere, a mouse screeched and scuttled across the rough wooden floor. Above Longarm's head, the ceiling creaked and groaned under shuffling feet, and he could hear the muffled cries of the pleasure girls cowering in their cribs.

Longarm ran across the room, leaping crates and weaving around barrels and vats, and bounded up five steps to a doorway beyond which the gunfire grew louder. He pushed through the door, cat-footed through a dim hall, mounted another set of steps.

He stopped when footfalls sounded above. Hinges creaked and wan light washed into the cavernlike stairwell. Longarm stepped into a doorless room. Pressing his left shoulder against the frame, he stood back in the shadows, peering into the stairwell from which the muted thunder o footsteps and muttered exclamations emanated.

"I knew it was coming to this," a girl said above the din o slapping feet and strained breaths.

"Oh, shut up, Yvette," said another girl. "You've earned damn good living here. It had to end sometime!"

"Fuck you, Marlene!"

"Both of you, shut up and move!" demanded another gir with an odd, squeaky voice.

As shadows appeared to his left, moving down the twist ing stairwell, Longarm moved deeper into the room. Per fume and talcum wafted from the hall. The floor jounce beneath Longarm's boots. The scrapes and slaps of ligh footsteps quickly died as the half-dozen whores made a hast retreat from the gunfire out the way Longarm had entered.

He moved out of the empty room and up the steps Ahead, a door stood half open. The shooting grew louder men barking orders back and forth, cartridges clinking an rolling on hardwood.

Longarm eased through the door and into a broad alcov housing several gambling tables and a roulette wheel. On th far side of the room, a billiard table sat beneath a shaggy mounted bison head. Out of sight to his left, several rifle and pistols barked furiously, and there was the scrape of table across the puncheons and the clatter of brass car tridges, as though someone had knocked a shell box onto th floor.

Longarm moved toward the din. The smell of rotten egg assaulted his nose and made his eyes water. Powder smok webbed the air. He moved down a short flight of step turned at the top of another, longer flight, and dropped int the saloon's main hall. The room was empty, the two fron windows shattered. Beyond, four men were hunkered dow on the porch, firing into the street. Another rifle boomed i the second story.

Longarm moved forward between the long, L-shaped ba on his left and the tables on his right. At the front of th room, he stopped before the broken window, dropped to on

182

knee to avoid bullets winging toward him from Friendly and his men on the street, and faced the porch where two dead men lay sprawled on the floor behind the four men shooting from behind an overturned table and a couple of beer barrels. They were big men who worked their weapons like professionals, and they were all dressed in suit pants, pin-striped shirts, vests, and bowler hats. The one on the far right end of the porch, shooting toward that end of the Dwarf House, puffed a cigar.

The dwarf himself was nowhere in sight. Could he be the shooter shooting from the room above?

Longarm thumbed his Winchester's hammer back and aimed the rifle straight out from his right shoulder.

"Federal law! Throw down your iron!"

The man with the cigar whipped his head toward the broken window behind him, long auburn hair flying about his shoulders. He dropped his cigar as he shouted, *"Fuck!"*

He swung his Henry rifle toward Longarm, but hadn't leveled the barrel before Longarm drilled him through the teeth. The others cursed and whipped around toward the lawman, who, working the Winchester's cocking lever and firing smoothly from one knee, laid them all out against the porch rail or sprawled over the edge of the overturned table in seconds.

Screams rose and blood geysered.

One man bounded to his feet, blood spewing from the hole in his chest, and Longarm fired again, punching him back over the railing. There was a wet thud as the man hit the street, his rifle clattering after him.

With the four shooters on the porch having been silenced, Friendly's men concentrated their gunfire on the upper-story window, from which the rifle shots became sporadic.

Longarm wheeled, ran to the back of the saloon, and took the steps three at a time. He bounded up another staircase and, keying on the rifle reports on the floor above, sprinted down a dim hallway, his boots thundering on the rough-cut pine planks.

The shots stopped, but not before Longarm had identified

the room the shooter was in. He stepped back from the door, then bounded forward, smashing his right boot flat against the left panel near the handle. The door flew open, spewing splinters. Ahead, a thick man in a frock coat—another thug, not the dwarf—stood silhouetted in the window, rifle extended toward the doorway.

Longarm bounded off his heels, diving straight into the room. The thick man's rifle boomed and the slug slammed into a door across the hall. Longarm hit the floor on his right shoulder. He came up firing one round and levering one more, but holding his finger taut against the trigger.

Before him he glimpsed the shooter's horror-stretched face as he tumbled backward through the window, firing another round into the ceiling as blood spewed from his wool vest like a small geyser. There was a screech of breaking glass and a thump as his boots scraped the windowsill, and then he was gone.

"Jesus *Christ*!" a man exclaimed.

Longarm turned to the bed right of the window. A paunchy, gray-bearded gent with salt-and-pepper hair cowered in the far corner with two pleasure girls. He and one of the girls had a sheet pulled up to their chests, while the other girl lay naked on the sheets, squirming and clawing at the man's arm as if she wanted to crawl between him and the wall.

They all stared at Longarm warily.

The girl under the sheets was sobbing.

"Where's the dwarf?" Longarm said, straightening. "Where the hell's the *dwarf*?"

"He certainly isn't in here!" The graybeard on the bed jerked the sheet a little higher while regarding Longarm as though he were an enraged bear that had wandered in.

Longarm cursed and stepped into the hall. Around him doors squawked partway open and male or female faces peeked into the hall. Two rooms down on his left, a young man in long silk underwear, derby hat, and half-boots stepped into the hall, angling toward Longarm, muttering under his breath. His thinly bearded cheeks were ashen, his eyes bright with worry.

"Is the judge all right?" he asked, his voice trembling. A young woman peeked through the door behind him, one breast and a bare leg revealed.

Longarm scowled at the young man. *"Judge?"*

"Judge Blackwood." The young man brushed past Longarm into the room Longarm had left.

The lawman laughed mirthlessly and moved off down the hall, asking the faces staring at him through cracked doors if they'd seen the judge. Heads shook or shoulders lifted in response, and a door slammed shut.

Longarm descended the stairs to the main hall as Friendly came in the front door followed by two deputies. Carrying a dusty, blood-splattered rifle that he must have picked up in the street.

"Nice shootin', Custis."

"You seen the dwarf?"

Friendly jerked a sharp look at him. "You didn't get him?"

Longarm wheeled toward the stairs. "The little fucker must be hidin' under a bed!"

He stopped abruptly. In his mind's ear, he heard the odd, squeaky voice he'd heard on the stairs when he'd first entered the building. *"Both of you, shut up and move!"*

That had been no girl's voice. It had been the pinched voice of a little man hustling out the back with the pleasure girls!

Longarm wheeled and ran to the front of the saloon hall, brushing past Friendly, who stared at him, incredulous.

He descended the porch stairs two steps at a time, breathing hard, the smell of cordite still thick in his nostrils. He glanced to his right, stopped suddenly halfway down the steps. Mary Lou was walking toward him from the jailhouse, holding a rifle over her right shoulder.

"Where's Amber?" Longarm called.

Mary Lou tossed her head toward the jailhouse. The door

185

was open. A short, squat shadow scampered out from the building's far corner. Holding a small pistol down by his belly, the dwarf scuttled into the jailhouse.

Mary Lou hadn't seen the dwarf. She'd turned back to Longarm, cocking her head and slitting her eyes. "You two on a first-name basis now, are—?"

"Christ!" Longarm muttered, leaping into the street.

He'd taken one stride when a scream rose from the jailhouse. He'd taken one more when a pistol popped. Longarm ran headlong past Mary Lou and the deputy and continued toward the jailhouse, pumping his arms and legs.

Reports emanated from the open jailhouse door as he got closer.

Longarm gritted his teeth as another scream cut the air. It was the same odd, squeaky voice he'd heard in the Dwarf House stairwell.

Another report sounded as he gained the jailhouse and pressed his left shoulder against the frame, edging a glance inside.

"Lasso that fuckin' bitch! Stop her!" The dwarf's crackling voice echoed off the stone walls. "She's gonna *kill* me!"

Longarm bolted into the office. Amber stood at the end of Friendly's desk, aiming a .36-caliber pistol toward the floor on the other side, where the dwarf was cowering in the corner, squirming around while shielding his face with his arms. A pistol lay on the floor near the doorjamb.

Longarm grabbed the girl's hand, jerking the gun up, another round plunking into the ceiling before he wrenched the weapon free of Amber's grip.

"Fuckin' biteh is tryin' to kill me!"

"You were trying to kill *me!"* Amber screamed, lunging toward the little man. "You brought me here, said you were gonna make me *famous,* then you tried to *kill me!"*

Longarm let her give the little man one good kick, then grabbed her arm and hauled her back to the other side of the desk. Mary Lou had run in behind Longarm, and now her father bolted through the door as well, his six-shooter in his hand.

Spying the dwarf in the corner, the sheriff grinned.

He glanced at Longarm as the dwarf continued cursing ie girl while clapping a hand to his bullet-grazed forehead.

Friendly looked around. "Who shot him?"

Longarm glanced at Amber, who crossed her arms on her hest as she continued staring with revulsion at the dwarf. If my aim had been better, he'd be *dead*!"

"All in good time, Miss Rogers," Friendly said as he hol- tered his Remington, then reached down and jerked the ursing dwarf to his feet. "It's gonna be a real treat to see his little demon kicking at the end of a long rope!"

Friendly shoved the dwarf across the room and into the cell e'd occupied before, and locked the door. Through the bars e said, "Dwarf, you're under arrest for murder, attempted nurder, disturbing the peace, smelling bad, looking ugly, and few other things I'll make up when I write up my report!"

The dwarf sagged back on his cot, clutching his forehead nd half crying, half squealing, "That fucking bitch killed ne! She done killed me, goddamn her hide!"

"Not yet," Longarm said. He ripped off his preacher's ollar, then shucked his handkerchief from his back pocket nd wrapped it around Amber's bloody forearm. "But as oon as those gallows are built . . ."

"Ain't gonna waste time on a gallows," Friendly groused. I already picked out a cottonwood down by the creek." He rinned. "Nice tall one with thick branches . . ."

"I think I'll stick around for the hanging." Amber winced s she watched Longarm wrap her arm. "Custis, will you tay too?"

"*Custis?*" Mary Lou stood by the door. She cocked one oot and canted her head at Longarm, still holding the rifle cross her shoulder.

Amber looked at her, frowning.

"Nah, I think I'll head on home," Longarm said with an nward grimace, cutting his eyes between the two women as iey locked accusatory stares with each other. "Very next ain, matter of fact . . ."